Wild Jack

Wild Jack

JOHN CHRISTOPHER

Aladdin

New York London Toronto Sydney New Delhi

ALADDIN

An imprint of Simon & Schuster Children's Publishing Division
1230 Avenue of the Americas, New York, NY 10020
This Aladdin paperback edition May 2015
Text copyright © 1974 by John Christopher
Cover illustration copyright © 2015 by Anton Petrov
Also available in an Aladdin hardcover edition.
All rights reserved, including the right of reproduction in whole or in part in any form.
ALADDIN is a trademark of Simon & Schuster, Inc.,
and related logo is a registered trademark of Simon & Schuster, Inc.
For information about special discounts for bulk purchases, please contact
Simon & Schuster Special Sales at 1-866-506-1949 or business@simonandschuster.com.
The Simon & Schuster Speakers Bureau can bring authors to your live event. For more information or to book an event contact the Simon & Schuster Speakers Bureau at
1-866-248-3049 or visit our website at www.simonspeakers.com.
Cover designed by Karin Paprocki
Interior designed by Hilary Zarycky
The text of this book was set in Venetian 301.
Manufactured in the United States of America 0415 OFF
2 4 6 8 10 9 7 5 3 1
Library of Congress Control Number 2015932420
ISBN 978-1-4814-2007-5 (hc)
ISBN 978-1-4814-2006-8 (pbk)
ISBN 978-1-4814-2008-2 (eBook)

To Wild Julia

I

I WOKE UP TO THE SOUND OF HUMMING, LIKE that of an enormous bee whose wings you might think filled the sky. I did not need to look at my watch to know it was eight o'clock. Today was Wednesday, and that was the Rome airship coming in to land.

Yawning, I stretched but did not get up right away. The windows facing my bed took up the full length of the wall, and I could lie and look out over the parks and buildings of London. In the foreground was the garden of our house, extending for more than a hundred yards in patterns of lawn and shrubbery, flower beds, and cunningly designed streams and pools. The gardeners were already at work.

Beyond, divided from the garden by a high fence covered with climbing roses, lay St. James's Park, at this time quiet and empty. In the distance I could just see a corner of the Palace, which was the seat of government for the city. My father was a member of the council, which met there, though at the moment he and my mother were away, on holiday in the Mediterranean.

In the opposite direction stood the huge funnel shape of the airport. The humming grew louder as the airship descended toward it, then cut off as it sank beneath the containing walls. I should not have heard it at all, of course, if my windows had not been opened—my room was sound-proofed and air-conditioned—but I rather liked the noise. I also liked waking to the smell of growing things, new-mown grass and flowers. The air-conditioner had a scent console incorporated in it which could have provided much the same effect, but I never thought it got things quite right.

The day was fine. Sunlight lit the scene outside and slanted through my windows, sharpening the blues and reds of the Persian carpet beside my bed. That was enough in itself to justify feeling cheerful, but I was aware of a sense of anticipation as well. I remembered: Miranda.

She was a cousin of mine, or, to be accurate, her father and mine were cousins. The Sherrins lived in Southampton, seventy miles from London. They had lived in London some years earlier, and Mr. Sherrin and my father had been political rivals. I knew nothing about the causes of their disagreement, but it had been serious. There had apparently been a lot of argument and debate, with people taking sides. In the end it had come to an issue in the council, where my father had won. To clinch matters, Mr. Sherrin's opponents had voted him into exile.

My father had not wanted that and in the years since then had worked to have the order of banishment revoked. He had succeeded a few months earlier. The Sherrins had not yet decided whether or not to return permanently to London, but my parents had suggested that they make use of our house while they themselves were away on holiday. So they had come up from Southampton and brought Miranda with them.

She was a few months younger than I, and I

remembered her as a thin plain girl with not a great deal to say for herself. I discovered she had changed a lot. She still did not talk much, though what she did say was in a cool low voice that made you want to listen. In other respects she was very different. Her hair was longer, silky, and more golden than I remembered, and her face was fuller, but with attractive hollows under high cheekbones. There was her smile, too, which was harder to describe: slow and strange. It was rare, but worth waiting for.

I decided to get up and pressed the button by my bed which would flash a call signal in the servants' quarters. It was very quiet now that the airship had landed, with only the small distant sounds of the gardeners. I wondered how many people had come from Rome: not many, probably. People did not travel much between the cities. Why should they, since one place was so much like another? There was no reason to leave one's home city except to go on holiday, and no one was likely to want to go on holiday to another city.

The bell on my door pinged softly and I called, "Come in." My manservant, Bobby, crossed the room to my bed.

"Good morning, young sir. I trust you slept well. What would you like for breakfast today?"

He listened and nodded as I gave my orders, then went to run my bath and put out my clothes to wear, asking me which shirt I preferred. Before leaving to fetch my breakfast, he said, "Is there anything else, young sir?"

I shook my head. "No, boy!"

Bobby had been my manservant since I came out of the nursery. He was more than three times my age.

White clouds drifted in from the west but the morning stayed bright, and after breakfast I took Miranda down to the river. Our boathouse on the Thames was close to the Houses of Parliament, which had once been the center of government but was now a museum. It was not much visited: I saw servant-attendants there, but no one else.

We met Gary at the boathouse. He and I were in the same class at school and slept in the same dormitory. We were friends after a fashion, though we did seem to spend a lot of time fighting. Usually I won. We were about the same height, but he was thinner than I was and less strong.

"You're late," he said.

That was true; Miranda had taken a long time getting ready. I paid no attention to him and led the way into the boathouse.

There were four boats in the slips. One was the family cabin cruiser, another was my father's speedboat, and a third belonged to my mother. The fourth was mine, a present for my last birthday. According to the regulations, I was not old enough to take a powerboat out on the river, but my father had managed to fix things for me.

It was an eight-foot dinghy, bright red, with a small but quite powerful motor. The boathouse servant made it ready, unplugging the powerline through which the batteries had been charged and connecting the batteries to the engine. He saluted me and handed over.

She was called "Sea Witch." I was not entirely satisfied with the name and thought occasionally of changing it. In the last day or two it had crossed my mind that "Miranda" might be a good name for a boat.

I eased her from the slip into the channel and so out of the boathouse into the river. With Miranda and Gary standing on either side of me, I opened up the throttle and took her down river. There were quite a lot of small craft about. Over the high-pitched hum of the engine I asked Miranda about Southampton: did people there do much boating?

She shook her head, the wind tumbling her yellow hair. "Not as much as here. Of course, there's much less river within the wall. The Outlands are nearer to us than they are to you."

"The Outlands" was the name for everything outside the boundaries of the cities and the holiday islands. There were roads running through them linking the civilized places, and the ground was kept clear for fifty yards or so on either side of the roads. Beyond that, nature ran riot, chiefly in forest.

Savages lived in the Outlands. They occasionally tried to attack cars on the roads, but usually without success since the cars traveled too fast to be damaged by a stone or two thrown by a few barbarians. If they attempted to mass in large numbers or put up barriers or obstacles, electronic monitors gave a warning to the nearest control unit. It was easy enough then to send an airship to deal with them.

But here we were in the heart of London, one of the biggest cities in the world, and the Outlands seemed very remote. On either bank of the Thames we saw buildings spaced among patches of green. I recalled a picture I had seen of Old London, with the houses packed close together, row on row of them, close-crammed and full of people—millions of people swarming like ants. Today we numbered ourselves in a few thousand. I tried to think about a million people—a thousand times a thousand—but it was beyond imagining.

In the distance, across open ground, I could see our house and even make out the small turret room which was my father's study. To the right was the airport funnel, with an airship at this moment rising out of it. That one was starting on the long route to Delhi. I knew the times of all the scheduled flights.

The energy tower stood farther to the right still, a slender shaft rising high into the sky. It was clad in anodized aluminum which reflected the sun so that it gleamed like a tower of gold—which in a way it was, because the energy tower generated and dispensed the power which kept the city alive. Everything depended on it: this small boat as much as the automat factories. The power line in the boat house ran back to the energy tower.

Airships had their own nuclear motors, but everything else came from the towers. The cars which traveled between the cities were powered by fuel cells which had to be charged at regular intervals. Each city had its own energy tower, but the London tower was the biggest in England.

I drove the boat between two pillars, the remains of an old bridge, and we came out into the wider stretch of the London docks. They had no use any longer; air freighters carried what trade there was in and out of the city.

It must have been a strange place in the old days, with the great ships rising high above the water, the air loud with the cries of stevedores, the clank of steel, the hoarse shrieks of steam whistles. We traveled now through silence and emptiness. I saw a solitary speedboat in the distance, that was all. Not many people came to this section of the river, disliking it for the bare wideness of its waters.

Gary held the same view and said so. This was boring. Why didn't we go to the pleasure gardens on the south bank? There would be something to do there.

I asked Miranda: "What do you think? Would you rather go to the pleasure gardens?"

She shook her head slightly. "I like it here."

I took the boat under high walls of gray stone, hiding the sun. We came to a flight of worn steps, and I tied up to a rusting metal ring. I helped Miranda out, and Gary and I followed her up the steps to the top. We came into sunshine again and sprawled on the warm stone, Gary and I carelessly and Miranda neatly. She was wearing lime-green trousers with a primrose-yellow blouse, and she hugged her knees with clasped hands.

I said: "I came here once on my own and stayed till after dark. It was a bit weird: the gray of the sky and the river getting darker all the time and no sound apart from the lap of waves and a seagull. I could almost imagine I saw a ghost liner coming in from the estuary."

"Some imagination." Gary laughed. "What a nut!"

Miranda said quietly, "I can understand that. It's a strange atmosphere, even in daylight." She smiled. "I don't think I would have had the nerve to stay here alone after dark."

"Two nut cases," Gary said. But he sounded more resentful than contemptuous.

· · ·

Mr. Sherrin appeared in the sitting room while I was waiting for Miranda that evening, and I put down the magazine I had been glancing through. He said, "That's all right, Clive. Don't let me interrupt you."

I shook my head. "I wasn't reading. Just passing the time."

The magazine was called *Twent-Cent* and carried stories and picture strips about the past, before the Breakdown. They were mostly lurid accounts of violence and crime, and at one time I had been keen on them. But one felt differently as one grew older; they were really meant for a younger age group than mine. I was a little ashamed of being found looking at the magazine at all.

Mr. Sherrin smiled. "Waiting for Miranda? You'll need plenty to occupy your time if you're going to make a habit of that."

He was tall and gray-haired, with a face that, except for being thinner, resembled my father's: both had bushy eyebrows and rather long noses. But there was also a difference in expression, which I suppose you might sum up by saying that my father was a laughing man, Mr. Sherrin a smiling one. His smile was quiet and humorous, seeming to indicate someone who took a cool look at people and situations and the world in general. It was a bit like Miranda's, when I came to think of it.

My father's laughter, on the other hand, appeared to stem from a greater energy and boisterousness. Quietness was characteristic of Mr. Sherrin, but my father was most himself in doing something or saying something—the latter generally loudly and to an accompaniment of expansive gestures. I had occasionally found this trying. It was not that I was ashamed of my father—I was very proud of him—but there had been moments when I wished he could go about things a little less noisily.

I made some fumbling reply to the remark about Miranda, and Mr. Sherrin said, "Where are you off to this evening, anyway? The theater?"

I shook my head. "Only a party."

"Anyone I know?" He smiled again. "I'm a bit out of touch with London society, of course."

The drily humorous comment was, I thought, typical of him.

I said, "Brian Grantham. His parents are away as well—in the Hebrides, I think."

"Michael Grantham would be his father?" I nodded. "Yes, I remember him."

He was silent after that. I wondered if Brian's
father had also been mixed up in the events leading
up to the banishment—and one of those, perhaps,
who had wanted the ban continued. But it wasn't
something I could ask questions about.

Miranda appeared at last and we could go. Mr.
Sherrin put music on as we left—Mozart or something similar. In my father's case it would have been
Tchaikovsky or more likely Gilbert & Sullivan. He
had an infuriating habit of whistling Sullivan tunes
off-key.

We took a taxi—open, because it was a clear warm
evening—to the Granthams' house, which was also
on the north bank but farther west—not far from
the wall, in fact. Brian, who had asked us, was at the
same school as Gary and I, but a couple of years
older. He had never invited either of us before, and
I was fairly sure I knew why he had done so this
time. The reason sat beside me, looking beautiful in
a crimson dress.

A dozen or more were there already, boys and

girls of Brian's age. There was the usual food and drink, dancing, and chatter. We were outside in the garden, and as the evening darkened, colored lamps lit up in the branches of trees all round. Occasionally there was also the light of a passing boat on the river. Music came from a number of speakers, and in quiet passages one could hear the splash of water.

We were drinking a light sparkling wine, and supplies ran out. A servant who looked about seventy came shuffling out with more. Someone called, "Get a move on, boy! We don't want to have to wait all night."

"Beg pardon, young sir."

He attempted to open a bottle with uncertain fingers, but the one who had spoken, Martin, said, "Leave it, boy, and totter away. I'll see to it."

The servant retreated, with another mumbled apology, and Martin started opening the bottle.

When the servant was out of earshot, Brian said, "Was that necessary?"

His voice was low but angry. Martin looked at him.

"What?"

"Talking that way to him. It's not his fault if he's old."

Martin laughed. "Perhaps not. Your parents' fault having him around, maybe. What's wrong with the rest home?"

The rest home was for old and sick servants, a kind of hospital. Food and shelter were provided, but not much in the way of extra comforts. There were usually plenty of vacancies; the servants who went there tended not to live very long.

"If you don't know," Brian said, "I don't suppose I could tell you." I was surprised how angry he was. "Anyway, he's our servant and I'll tell him what to do. And I don't like hearing him called 'boy.'"

Martin stared at him. "What's got into you? They're always called 'boy.'"

"Then it's about time they weren't. They're human beings, like us."

"Like us? Sure. Maybe we should fetch and carry for them, turn about. And have one or two of them on the council."

There was some laughter.

Brian said, "It might not be a bad idea, at that. What right do we have to make them serve us?"

The laughter stopped; I imagine the others were as shocked as I was. The division between masters and servants was something we had taken for granted all our lives—something you did not even need to think about. Nor want to. A remark like that gave one an uncomfortable, crawly feeling. Brian had probably drunk too much wine, but that didn't justify it. Martin merely turned away, and no one else said anything. We all wanted to drop the subject, but Brian insisted on going on.

"Have you ever thought about how they came to be servants in the first place?"

Martin turned back and looked at him in exasperation. He said dismissively, "What needs thinking about? Because they're descendants of savages, that's why. They wanted to come into the cities to get away from the Outlands, and our ancestors let them. In the Outlands they would be just about scraping a miserable living if they weren't killed by wild beasts first. With us they have food and clothing and shelter. They made the bargain."

"Their great-grandfathers made the bargain," Brian said. "Does that bind them?"

The question was too absurd to need an answer.

Brian went on, "And what about the time before that—before there were savages at all?"

"They've always been savages."

"No, they haven't. Only since the Breakdown."

Martin shrugged. Before the Breakdown were the Dark Ages—millennia of squalid barbarism, followed by the two centuries of the technological explosion which were as bad if not worse. We all knew that. For two hundred years mankind, suddenly given machines and power, had squandered the resources of energy, burning up coal and oil recklessly, with no thought for the future. Then the oil supplies had failed and the coal seams had become too thin for economic working. As a result the complex structure of the early twenty-first century had fallen apart in wars and rebellions and men fighting for crusts of bread among rusting machines.

People had died in the millions and tens of millions. Only a handful—*our* ancestors—had had the courage and determination and intelligence to start building again in the midst of chaos. The organizers had been those scientists with an understanding of the techniques of nuclear energy. They knew that although it had been inadequate in keeping the whole world with its billions of inhabitants running, it could be used to power dividual strongholds. So, one by one, the cities rose again, though far fewer and smaller, each centered about its energy tower. Beyond their walls stretched the Outlands, abandoned to the murderous whims of nature.

Brian seemed blind and deaf to the effect he was having. He said, "The reason the people of the Outlands became savages was because they were kept out of the cities. If they could have come in, they would have, and lived civilized lives. Those who tried were driven away, slaughtered."

"But if they had been let in," a girl said, "things would have been impossible. Everything was balanced on a knife edge. Any increase in numbers would have meant civilization breaking down again and us all becoming savages. Is that what you think should have happened?"

"There was a case for exclusion *then*," Brian said. "I'm not disputing that. But what about later? What about now? We have more food, more energy, more everything than we need. The cities could support ten times as many people as they do."

"So we could live in mobs again, like in the twentieth century?" That was another boy, Roland. "Let's bring the savages in and live alongside them in tenement buildings—is that what you want?"

"No, of course I don't." Brian suddenly seemed to realize the absurdity into which his argument had led him, and looked uncertain. "Anyway, I was talking about servants, really. They've lived in the cities for generations. We call them servants, but if we were honest we would call them slaves. They're born in slavery, live in slavery, die in slavery. In ancient Rome slaves had a slim chance of getting their freedom. Our servants have no hope at all."

There was a general murmur of disgust. The reference to ancient Rome had something to do with it. No one was interested in the Dark Ages, either early or late. And it wasn't true about slavery. Servants were paid money for their work—not a lot, it was true, but too much, many said, for the amount they did. "Slave" was an unpleasant expression which had no place in the civilized world of the twenty-third century.

Martin said, "You're just talking rubbish, Brian. The servants don't mind being servants, any more than the savages mind being savages. They're used to it—contented, in fact."

Brian asked, "How do you know?"

Roland said, "*I* know something. I know I've had enough of this talk. I mind that. Let's have some more music."

"You won't think," Brian said. "None of you will. That's the trouble—you won't let yourselves think."

"I'll tell you what I think," Martin said. "I think you should shut up, Brian, or else do the thing properly and go out and join Wild Jack."

That raised a laugh. We could all remember being told stories about Wild Jack by our nurses when we were little: Wild Jack, the bogeyman who would creep up from the Outlands, steal over the wall by night, and take back naughty children to his lair among the savages. Martin's remark reduced the subject to the level of the ridiculous, which was its proper place. Brian made a feeble attempt to continue with his protests, but no one was listening any longer.

After all, what point was there in talking about the Dark Ages or the savages, far away either in time or space? Servants brought out more food and drink. The sky was black above, but the lamps shone gaily in the trees. It was still warm, but if the evening were to turn cold, thermostats would switch on the heaters. A long boat, lit up from stem to stern, drifted past on the river, and farther off I heard the high whine of a speedboat.

The Outlands, we knew, were wild and trackless, inhabited by hungry, murdering savages, but all that was on the far side of the wall. We were snug in the city. I saw a high light in the distance, marking the summit of the energy tower.

Someone had turned up the music, and couples joined together to dance. Brian had seemingly accepted defeat and now had other things in mind. He came over and asked Miranda for a dance.

She gave him a small, cool smile. "I'm sorry. Clive's already asked me."

I hadn't, in fact, but I didn't argue about that. I took her out onto the circle of polished wood, laid down by the servants between the trees. For the first time I felt there had been some point in the grinding tedium of dancing lessons. She danced lightly, humming in tune to the music. It was good to hold her and see her face close to mine in the lamplight.

2

M Y PARENTS VISIPHONED FROM RHODES the day before the Sherrins went back to Southampton. The setting was middle distance so they were both on screen, with a view behind them of crumbling stone walls and the blue waters of the Mediterranean. They asked me how things were, and I told them fine.

My mother said, "I've talked your father into taking a yacht and exploring some of the smaller islands, so we shall be out of touch for a week or so. Will you be all right?"

I nodded. "Of course. It's a great idea."

My father said, "It means getting back to school on your own."

He sounded a bit anxious, but he tended to be about things like that. They were very different in temperament. She was quieter, more reserved, and more willing to give me credit for being able to look after myself.

I said, "That's OK. Bobby will see to everything. He's already started my packing."

We talked for a while, or rather my father did, telling me about Rhodes and the various things they had been doing. I got the impression it had been either sightseeing or sitting in the sun with a glass of something long and cool: not exactly my best notion of a holiday but obviously they were enjoying it. Later my father wanted to have a word with Mr. Sherrin, and I had him called and adjusted the visiphone to get him in alongside me. He thanked my father for the use of the house, and my father asked him how things had gone in London. "Reasonably well," he said, smiling. I guessed that could be politics.

After we had said good-bye and closed contact, Mr. Sherrin said, "I'm glad your father is having a good rest. He needs one. He drives himself very hard."

"Yes, I know."

"Not like me." Mr. Sherrin smiled. "I believe in taking things easy. By the way, I thought we might all go out for a meal this evening, since it's our last night. That place that's opened in the old Tower of London might be worth trying."

"Sure," I said. "Great."

The Sherrins had come up from Southampton by airship, and the following morning I went to the airport with them to see them off. Mr. and Mrs. Sherrin sat drinking coffee while they were waiting, and I managed to get Miranda away on the excuse of getting soft drinks from the dispenser.

I said, "It's been great having you here. Pity you have to go back so soon."

She shrugged, smiling. "Yes. There it is, though. School tomorrow."

"Yes. Me, too. Can I call you there?"

She shook her head. "No outside calls except in emergencies. And then we have a teacher sitting in on them."

"Can I write you?"

"If you want to."

"I do."

"Good." She smiled again. "I'll write back. I was wondering. . . ."

"What?"

"Whether it might be possible for you to come down and stay with us in the next holidays."

"Yes! I mean, if you're sure, I'd love to."

"I'll fix it. Look who's here."

I turned and saw Gary coming toward us. He had known, of course, that the Sherrins were leaving this morning, but I had deliberately not suggested his coming along. My greeting was chilly. He was chilly back, and concentrated on talking to Miranda. For the five minutes that remained before they were called we battled through a two-sided conversation, with Miranda having to cope with both channels. She did it very well, smiling at us in turn.

When it came to good-byes, though, she shook hands with Gary but offered me her cheek, which I kissed clumsily but triumphantly. Then she and her parents went up the ramp into the airship, appearing a moment or two later at one of the observation windows. We waved to her, and she waved back.

The airship's engine hummed and it started to lift off. We watched it, still waving. I could not resist saying, "Miranda's asked me to stay with them in the next holidays."

Gary did not respond right away. He said at last, "There's something quite remarkable about you."

Apart from anything else, his tone made it clear that was not intended as a compliment. I said, with an edge to my own voice, "Oh, yes?"

"It's what you think about yourself, that's all. You really do think you're terrific. Look at me—I'm Clive Anderson. Look at my red speedboat. Look at me driving it even though I'm underage, because my father fixed it with the license department. Look at my father, he's on the council. Look at my personal manservant. Look at my new power bike. Look at the size of my allowance."

I was annoyed, but grinned. "No, don't look at me—look at you. You're pathetic. You really are."

He swung at me. I wasn't ready and he knocked me off balance. I grabbed at a chair and it collapsed under me; a table went over, too. I got up and charged at him. We fought until a uniformed figure, an airport policeman, pushed us apart.

He was squat and fair-haired, very powerfully built, and the grip of his fingers on my shoulder hurt.

He said, "You know the regulations about brawling in public." He let go of me and picked up the chair, which had a broken leg. "Not to mention damaging city property. I think we'd better have you two on report."

He took out his memocorder, while Gary and I stared at him in silence, but instead of switching on he looked at me more closely.

"Aren't you Clive Anderson?"

"Yes, sir."

"Councillor Anderson's son?"

"Yes, sir."

He gave me another long look. "All right. We'll forget about it this time." He put the memocorder away. "Don't let it happen again."

He gave Gary a quick, uninterested glance before walking off. Gary and I went toward the exit without speaking. He didn't thank me for getting him off a report, but I didn't really expect him to. We went in opposite directions when we got outside.

• • •

Our school was in the north of the city, on the edge of Regent's Park, and during term we lived in. The dormitories each had twelve beds. Gary's bed and mine had been next to each other, but when we went back he moved to one at the far end of the room. That suited me perfectly well.

There was the usual confusion of settling in, with plenty to occupy one's time. We also had the results of our last set of examinations. This was one field in which Gary usually beat me comfortably, but on this occasion, by some freak, I wound up second in class, while he was fourth. Our form teacher said, "Very good work, Anderson. I congratulate you. Let's see if you can keep it up."

Gary's desk was a few feet from mine. I saw him out of the corner of my eye, trying not to look sick.

On the third day of term we were doing English when the teacher's visiphone buzzed. He accepted the call and the screen on his desk lit up. He used an earphone so we could not hear what was said, but I could tell he was surprised: He closed contact, and said, "Anderson!"

I stood up.

"Report to the headmaster's office."

I was surprised, too. I had never known the head-master call a boy out of a lesson before. I said, "You mean now, sir?"

"Yes, now."

The headmaster was called Weatherby, a tall thin man with a long thin face. Discipline in the school was fairly strict, but that was generally regarded as being due to his second in command, a small, tough, dark man called Williams. Williams was with him in his office, and so was a man I'd never seen before—as short as Williams but fatter, and wearing police uniform.

Weatherby said, "What have you been up to, Anderson?"

"Up to, sir?"

"You must have been up to something." He looked helpless. "They apparently want to see you at police headquarters. We haven't been given a reason."

He looked at the man in uniform, and the man in uniform looked stolidly back. I tried to think of a possible reason myself. I had not been in any trouble I knew of, except for that fight at the airport. Even if the airport policeman had changed his mind and decided to report me after all, it wasn't enough to justify something like this. And what about Gary? The policeman couldn't have reported me without reporting him.

I shook my head. "It must be a mistake."

Williams looked baffled, too, but in his case angry. He said sharply to the officer, "You do know this boy is Councillor Anderson's son? Surely they gave you some idea why he's wanted?"

The man shrugged. "I was only told to bring him."

Weatherby said, "You have the authority, so I suppose it's all right." He looked at me in a depressed way. "You'd better go with him, Anderson. I hope they don't keep you long. I can't think why these things can't be seen to outside school hours."

In the police car I tried to make conversation with my escort, in the hope of picking up a clue. Some of my friends were scared of the police, but they had never made me nervous. I had been used to seeing them around my father, of course, all my life. This one was civil, but uncommunicative. When we reached the police building, I knew as little of the reason for my being there as when we started.

I was quite familiar with the ground layout of the building, but my escort called the lift and took me to uncharted territory on the seventh floor. He left me with the duty officer, who dialed a number on his control panel, listened to an instruction, and motioned me to follow him. He took me to an office, halfway along a corridor, which we reached through one of a dozen identical doors.

There were two men in the office, which had windows overlooking St. James's Park. They were not wearing uniforms, but casual clothes. Both were quite young, neither over thirty, one narrow-shouldered and red-haired, the other dark and brawny.

The brawny one said, "Clive Anderson—that right?"

"Yes, sir."

He leaned back in his chair and stared at me thoughtfully. "Like to tell us all about it?"

"About what?"

He tilted his chair farther and sank his chin on his chest. "Come on, now. You know all right."

"I don't. I've no idea why I'm here."

Both watched me. Neither said anything.

I said at last, "I really don't understand, sir. But I think it might be a good idea if I could speak to Mr. Richie, my father's secretary. My father is Councillor Anderson."

The brawny one made a clicking sound with his tongue but did not straighten up. He said, "Yes, we know your father is Councillor Anderson. At the moment cruising among the Greek islands, I believe. Very pleasant, though I'm sure well-earned. As to Mr. Richie, we know where to get hold of him if we want him. There's no hurry about that. We'll finish our little chat with you first."

I disliked him, but I was not alarmed. The job of the police was to serve the city, and particularly the council.

I said, "I don't see that I can be much help when I haven't the faintest idea what the chat is supposed to be about."

"Don't be pert, boy." I stayed silent. "Do you know Brian Grantham?"

"Yes. He goes to my school."

I realized as I spoke that I had not seen him since the beginning of the new term. Not that that meant much, since he was not in my class or dormitory.

The policeman said, "Did you visit his house on"—he leaned forward and glanced at a pad in front of him—". . . on the evening of the sixteenth?"

That was the evening of the party. I said, "Yes."

"Who else was present?"

There seemed no point in not telling him. I reeled off the names I remembered. He nodded.

"What were the subjects of conversation?"

I began to feel wary. "I can't remember." I paused, but he waited for me to go on. "Well, all sorts of things. Football, boating . . . the new show at the Metrodome."

He nodded again. "And servants? And the savages?"

I shook my head. "I don't remember that."

"Don't you? What a pity. Let's see if we can do something about refreshing your memory. The part we're interested in started with someone addressing a servant as 'boy.' Nothing unusual, but I gather you objected to it."

"No! It was . . ."

"What?"

I couldn't say it was Brian who had objected. Quite obviously someone was taking all this more seriously than one would have thought, which meant in turn that someone might be in trouble. I wondered again about not seeing Brian in school this term. But the ridiculous thing was that I was being accused of saying it. Who could possibly have told them that? Brian himself? It didn't make sense.

I said, "It was a big party—twenty or more of us—and we were in the garden. I didn't hear everything that was said. All I can tell you is that I didn't make any objections to anything."

The policeman came forward in his chair, picked up his pad, and studied it. "You went on to give quite a little speech, it seems. Principally about the rights of servants. You said they were being treated as slaves and something ought to be done about that. The savages, as well. They had as much right to the benefits of the energy towers as we did. We ought to invite them into the cities—share and share alike." He looked up at me. "You appear to hold very strong views for your age."

I was terribly confused. This was a potted and garbled version of Brian's talk. Someone had informed on him to the police, at the same time twisting his words. But not on him, in fact—on me. I was the one being accused of it all.

The brawny man said in a more reasonable tone, "You just tell us all about it. We'll do what we can to make things easy for you."

It was ridiculous, but it was also starting to get worrying. The overwhelming majority of servants were contented and well-behaved. Very occasionally there would be one who caused trouble, most likely through some mental disturbance. Those who did were taken away by the police, to a hospital presumably. It was not a subject that interested me nor that I knew much about. Nothing like that had ever happened among our servants.

But I realized that the police might hold the view that the sort of talk Brian had gone in for would have an unsettling effect on servants who happened to overhear it—and that therefore it was something that ought to be stopped. But although that seemed reasonable, it didn't explain how I came into the picture. I hadn't made any contribution at all to the conversation; yet clearly someone had told the police I had. Why?

Or, equally important, who? Not Brian, ce... he would have only been landing himself i... Martin or Roland? But they, like Brian, to me in school, and I had had even less contact with them than with him. They had no reason to have a grudge against me.

What was becoming obvious was that I needed help. I said, "I'd like to speak to Mr. Richie."

"Yes." The policeman nodded. "You'll be able to do that. As soon as you've made a complete and proper statement to us."

"I've nothing to say."

He stared at me without speaking. The ginger-haired one still did not say anything either but began rubbing his hands together in a slow twisting way which I found unsettling.

I tried to think clearly. It was not as though the whole thing were fabricated. The notes on the pad were based on the actual talk that evening, though Brian's words had been twisted to sound worse. So information must have come from one of those present, and presumably someone who wanted to get me into trouble. Not Brian. Not Martin or Roland. Then who?

Suddenly I remembered catching sight of Gary as I left the classroom. Could that have been a look of triumph on his face?

There had always been some resentment, but it had been more in evidence recently. Although he had gone out in the speedboat with me, he had not been able to resist occasional snide remarks. Then there had been his jealousy over Miranda. Could he have figured out this way of getting back at me? The more I thought about it, the more certain I was.

I cried, "Gary Jones, isn't it?" They looked at me in silence. "It was Gary Jones told you all this. But it's all lies!"

The brawny one said, "We're not interested in Gary Jones. It's you we're interested in. And you'll be a lot better off telling the truth."

Knowing it was Gary, I felt better. An enemy you can identify is easier to cope with than the unknown. And that reassurance put the whole thing in different perspective. Even if they refused to call Mr. Richie in now, they could not keep him out of things indefinitely. For that matter, my father would soon be back in touch, and I could imagine his fury when he found out how I had been treated.

Everything would be properly gone into, not in a little office room with two idiot policemen but under the scrutiny of the council. And when that happened, the truth must come out, because others who were present at the party would be called as witnesses. They would testify I hadn't said anything.

I felt sorry for Brian, who if he wasn't already in trouble would probably be in it then. But the real load was going to fall on Gary; he was in for it once the truth came out. I didn't feel sorry for him, though I did feel contempt along with anger. He had been a fool as well as treacherous.

For my own part, I needed do nothing but wait. I said, "I'm not saying anything. Call Mr. Richie. I'll talk if he's present, not otherwise."

Some of my contempt—for these two as well—may have shown in my voice. The red-haired policeman spoke for the first time, in a thin, dry voice: "We aren't going to get anything out of him at this stage."

The other gave a questioning look and got a nod in reply. He pressed a button, and the duty officer came in from the corridor.

He said, "All right. Take him away."

On the ground floor I was handed back to the man who had brought me from school. There was a hitch then—something to do with the police car—and I noticed a public visiphone not far from the main desk. I went toward it, feeling in my pocket for a coin, but my escort called me back.

"What do you think you're doing?"

"Just making a call."

"Not allowed. Come back here."

I shrugged and obeyed. There were telephones at school which I could use to call Mr. Richie. The delay made no real difference.

As the car pulled away from the police building, I thought about Gary. True enough, he would get it in the neck when this was sorted out, but I wasn't in the mood for waiting that long. I felt very much like pitching into him the moment I got back into the classroom. No, I decided—better wait till after school. I didn't want any interruptions.

We turned a corner, and I said, "You're going the wrong way."

He did not answer, though he had clearly heard me. I was more curious than anything else. The route we were taking led to my father's office, where Mr. Richie worked. Perhaps they had had the sense to change their minds and refer it to him after all.

But the airport came first, and that was where the

police car drove in. A flash of a badge took us through to the departure lounge. Passengers were embarking on a civil airship at one of the main ramps. I was taken to a smaller ramp, farther on. A small gray airship was waiting there, a police craft.

I said, "Where am I supposed to be going?"

He didn't answer that either.

The airship took off almost immediately, rising past the civil aircraft, which was still loading. I had identified that one automatically: the 4:30 to Paris. We lifted to a couple of hundred feet before turning south. The river lay beneath us, dotted with small boats, and I saw the energy tower, the Houses of Parliament museum, a glimpse of my own home. Then the wall was under us and after that the waving green of close-packed trees.

We traveled southwest, cruising at about five hundred feet. I had a good view of the forest, for what it was worth. It stretched away, dense and featureless, in every direction.

Even with sunlight on it, it had a sinister look. There was no way of knowing what lay behind that green facade. Savages, certainly, and wild beasts. The flora and fauna of the Outlands were unknown—no one was interested, anyway—and books describing conditions before the Breakdown would not have helped much. Things must have changed a great deal. One of the barbarities of the Dark Ages had been the keeping of wild animals, from all over the world, in cages in what they called zoos. During the Breakdown many had escaped and bred in the wild. There were servants' stories, handed down from their great-grandfathers who had been savages, of lions, monkeys, wolves. The forests might conceal anything.

And, of course, there were the savages themselves. I thought, more with irritation than anything else, of Brian's stupid ramblings. They had been the cause of all this. Really stupid. The savages were in their proper place down there, where they ought to be.

We went on southwest, and I wondered again about our destination. Southampton, perhaps? I couldn't think why it should be, but it was the next city on this route. The white of buildings glimmered in the distance, and my spirits rose. I was in favor of Southampton, whatever the reason. Miranda was at school, but there might be some chance of seeing her. I could certainly call on Mr. Sherrin for any help I needed.

The buildings grew larger and took on shape. I saw the long sweep of the wall and the energy tower. But there was no indication of our losing height for a descent. The airship passed over the town, still at five hundred feet, and went on. Forest was replaced by sea beneath us: deep blue, smooth from this height, with nothing moving on it. It looked even more depressing than the forest.

We were heading out of England, and I began to be worried. I told myself it made no difference. In every country cities formed part of the network of civilization. Mr. Richie would have no difficulty in finding the son of Councillor Anderson and bringing him back to London.

The thing to do, I decided, was to treat it as an interesting break from school. Even looking at the dreary sea was better than fuel technology with Mr. Harper.

I was thinking that when the engine note deepened; we were going down. Surely not into the sea? I looked more closely and saw it below, very small but land certainly. An island.

3

WE STOOD, GOOSE-PIMPLED, IN LONG LINES on the parade ground. The sun was shining but there was a chilly wind from the northeast. It was a windy island altogether; according to Kelly it had not stopped blowing in the six months he had been here.

Kelly was American and felt the cold; his home city was Jacksonville, Florida. He had brown eyes and brown hair, a brown lazy look to him in general. He preferred sitting to standing and lying to sitting and took catnaps at every opportunity. But the impression he gave was misleading, as I had discovered on my first evening in camp.

The camp consisted of tents pitched in what had once been a field but was now just beaten earth. Each tent housed about twenty boys, and on arrival I had been given a couple of blankets and escorted to one of them. My first shock was realizing I was supposed to sleep there and that there were no beds, only the bare ground.

When the guard had gone, the other boys started asking questions: who was I, where did I come from? I wasn't feeling very sociable. I was confused and uncertain, and my intention of treating the whole thing as an amusing break from school routine was somewhat blunted by the prospect of the night ahead. My bed at home was air-sprung, silk-sheeted, temperature-controlled, and had a TV screen fitted into the foot. I looked from my blankets to the scuffed earth of the tent floor with no enthusiasm at all.

So I was short in my answers, possibly rude, which did not go down very well. Questions turned to comments on my appearance and behavior, and the comments rapidly became pointed. A sharp-faced, fair-haired boy mimicked my voice in an exaggerated accent. I told him to shut up, and he mimicked that, too. Then I hit him.

He went sprawling across the tent, cannoning into others. Two of his friends went for me together, and he got back on his feet and joined in. It wasn't long before I was on the ground myself, with one of them kicking me.

Up to this point Kelly had been lying on his blankets some distance away, presumably asleep. He went into action very fast; he had scattered them by the time I realized what was happening. I got up and we stood side by side. They looked at us and after a moment's hesitation retreated, grumbling.

I put a hand out. "Thanks a lot."

"No sweat."

We exchanged names and afterward chatted. I felt better after the fight, less on edge. Kelly made one of the other boys move up so that I could lay out my blankets next to his and showed me how to arrange them for maximum warmth. He told me, with feeling, that it got cold in the small hours.

I didn't at that point realize just how lucky I had been in falling in with Kelly and being befriended by him. The blankets on the other side of his belonged to his friend Sunyo, and the pair had established a strong ascendancy inside the tent. No one was anxious to interfere with them, and being accepted as a third member of the alliance gave me a share in the prestige.

Sunyo, Kelly told me, was Japanese, from Kyoto. I looked around for a yellow skin and slant eyes, but Kelly shook his head.

"He's outside somewhere."

"Outside?" The tent was full and people were clearly settling down for the night. "Is that allowed?"

Kelly shrugged. "They don't bother to restrict our movements when we're not working or on parade. There's no reason why they should; after all, we're stuck on the island. There are caves you could hide in, and you might try living on rabbits and seagulls— raw—if you could catch them. Not for long, though. The food in the camp is terrible, but it keeps you alive. You would have to come back when you were starving, and then you'd get the stockade."

"The stockade?"

He pulled a face. "Let's not talk about that, not right now anyway. No, Sunyo's just gone outside to meditate."

Again I repeated his word, idiotically: "Meditate?"

Kelly grinned. "We're both fond of sitting down—I guess you could say it's a bond. But Sunyo uses it to contemplate life at a higher level, while all I do is think about getting out of here, getting a proper meal, taking a tub. I settle for a few minutes' sleep. The higher life requires a bit more privacy."

Sunyo came back not long after, and Kelly introduced us. I had been expecting someone thin and pale, spiritual-looking, but he proved to be short and squat, heavily muscled. The strength of his grip impressed me. He had broad features, at first sight ugly but later interesting, their expression oddly balanced between an appearance of great control and one of latent, maybe wild energy.

Now, the day after, I stood between them on the parade ground and listened to the commandant. He was a very big man with a very florid face. The island guards wore standard gray police uniforms, though with different shoulder insignia. The commandant's uniform was gray, too, but heavily braided with gold at the shoulders and cuffs and along the peak of his cap.

He had a plummy voice, which switched between a note of insincere good will and bursts of braying indignation. It started on the first.

"We have one or two new boys on parade today."
He opened his red face in a cavernous smile. "So I
think it might be a good idea to talk about the purpose of this island training school. Most of you will
have heard it before. I hope you are going to bear
with me and listen patiently again."

One of the boys shifted an inch or so, and a
guard moved in his direction, his baton raised. The
commandant paid no attention and went on.

"Training school, I say. Some people call it a punishment school, but this is the term I prefer.
Punishment, after all, is negative; training positive. It
has purpose, an objective. What is that objective?
Quite simply, to produce good citizens. Good citizenship is the most important quality any human being
can have, because society itself depends on it.

"Think," he said, "—think for a moment of our
forefathers."

He paused to let us think. While we were doing
so, a guard bellowed, "You at the back there! Stand
up straight!"

"Our forefathers," the commandant said, "were
great men. In a dark and dying world they carried the
torch of civilization. While everything else was crum-

bling and falling, they built the cities in which we now live—the cities in which all of you were born. If they had been selfish, willful men, none of that could have been achieved. The whole world would have collapsed into the barbarism of the Outlands. But they were not selfish or willful; they were good citizens.

"Because of them you—all of you—were born into a decent and civilized life rather than the brutish life of the savages, continually threatened by hunger, disease, death in a thousand forms. You only have to look across the wall of your city to see what might have been. It is something to be humbly grateful for."

His voice took on an edge, the beginning of the bray. "Most young people are grateful. They obey the mild and sensible rules laid down for their good by their elders. Only a small and wretched minority cause trouble. They are the boys who put self before citizenship, their own whims before the needs of society.

"Few, as I say, but that does not mean they are unimportant. Small patches of rottenness, if left unchecked, can infect and eventually destroy everything. But we are not going to let that happen. The way we are going to prevent it is by cutting out the rottenness from individuals before it can spread to the rest of the community, to those who are still healthy.

"That is the reason for your being here. All of you have shown by your behavior that you are part of the corruption I am talking about. And that corruption must be destroyed before it destroys the good life we have inherited!"

His voice had been rising. He paused, and resumed in his quieter, unctuous tone: "We must look on the bright side. You can be cleansed and rescued. No one is beyond redemption. It may take a long time, perhaps a very long time, but we can make you into decent citizens. I promise you that, and I promise you something else: not one of you will leave this island till that end has been achieved.

"How shall we do it? First, by deprivation. Deprivation of all the good things—family, rich foods, leisure, amusements—which you had and did not value. Secondly, by work. Our forefathers worked unstintingly in building the cities after the Breakdown. You will work as hard or harder. And work will drive from your minds the folly and selfishness which brought you here.

"You have heard something of the hard and ugly lives of the savages. Your lives, too, will be hard and ugly. There will be room in your minds for one thought only—how to get away, how to get back to the city whose warmth and comfort and security you failed to appreciate when you had them. And how are you to achieve it? I can put it in one word: obedience—obedience not just from the mouth but from the heart."

He was working up to the bray again. "The guards will teach you obedience. Those of you who have any sense will cooperate with them. The quicker you learn, the quicker you go home. I advise you not to show slackness in this lesson. However unpleasant your life may seem at the moment, rest assured that it can be made worse. Much worse! Here on the island our power is absolute, and we shall not hesitate to use it! Either you return to your homes as good citizens, worthy of your forefathers, or you never return at all. Never!"

That was almost a shriek. He turned to one of the officers and said in a quieter voice, "Dismiss the parade. Form work parties."

There was no opportunity for talking to Kelly and Sunyo until after supper, a meal consisting of watery stew and hunks of stale gray bread. I had been wondering about the rest of the boys—five hundred or more of them. Presumably they had all been in trouble at home. I also wondered about Kelly and Sunyo and asked them.

Kelly's difficulties had started in school. He had not been, he admitted, the most industrious of pupils; work for its own sake did not appeal to him. The one thing he was interested in was history, particularly the history of the American empire, which had dominated the twentieth century. But in Jacksonville, as in London, history was not taught as a subject and was very much discouraged as an interest.

By refusing to pay much attention to the subjects that were taught, Kelly naturally annoyed his teacher. But he made things worse by being clever enough to pick things up and do well in examinations, which maddened the teacher even more. A feud developed between them and gradually grew in bitterness, the teacher continually looking for new ways of getting at Kelly and Kelly doing his best to make the teacher look a fool in return.

They might have carried on in this way indefinitely, or at any rate until Kelly switched teachers, but for the presence of another boy in the class. His school work was bad, too, but he lacked Kelly's cleverness. The teacher picked on him at first in an ordinary way, but then realized that he was a friend of Kelly's and that Kelly got angry on his behalf. Recognizing the weak spot, the teacher exploited it to the full. Ignoring Kelly completely, he concentrated on harrying the other.

Things came to a head when the boy turned in a particularly bad paper in an examination. The rule was that a boy could not be beaten for bad work, but he could for insolence. The teacher took, or said he took, the view that the work had been scamped intentionally, as an act of impertinence, and caned him in front of the class. Kelly stuck it for six strokes, then got up from his seat and wrenched the cane from the master's hand. There was a struggle, which wound up with Kelly caning the master.

The school authorities took the view that the breach of discipline was too serious to be dealt with by them. Kelly was referred to the police, and the police sent him to the island.

Sunyo's story was different, though there were points of resemblance. He came from a Japanese family which traced its ancestry back beyond the

Breakdown to an ancient nobility. The rulers of Kyoto, like the rulers of other cities, approved of venerating our forefathers of the Reconstruction but strongly disapproved of anyone taking an interest in people who lived in the Dark Ages.

Sunyo's father followed the ancient religion of Shinto and had a shrine in the garden of his house hung with pictures of his ancestors. The Kyoto Council condemned this and ordered the shrine to be pulled down and the pictures destroyed. When Sunyo's father defied them, they sent police to do it.

As a result, Sunyo's father committed suicide by the traditional rite of hara-kiri. Sunyo himself was not a Shintoist, but he had loved and revered his father and he held the police responsible for his death. He collected together a band of boys who called themselves samurai, after the knights of old Japan, and they declared a kind of guerrilla war on the authorities. This culminated in a raid on the police building itself, during which they broke windows and smeared slogans on the walls with paint.

Some of them were caught, and one betrayed Sunyo, naming him as the leader. The others were punished locally, but Sunyo was sent to the island.

They asked me about myself, and I told them. They were both incredulous.

"Just because of talk?" Kelly said. "And you didn't even do the talking."

Sunyo said, "Surely they ought to have made a proper investigation before sending you to a place like this."

I shrugged. "Somebody made a mistake, I suppose."

"And your father's a councillor?"

"Yes, but he's away at present. And they wouldn't let me visiphone his secretary. When he does get back, he'll clear it up pretty quickly."

"And then some policeman will be in trouble," Sunyo said with satisfaction. "Probably more than one."

"At any rate," Kelly said, "it doesn't look as though you're going to be with us for long."

I said, "I hope not," without thinking, then regretted the words. Neither of them had any prospect of getting away for a very long time.

I had spoken to two of the guards and asked to be allowed to see the commandant. The first treated the request as an impertinence and warned me that if I persisted in that sort of thing I was going to find myself in front of him in circumstances I should not like. The second guard was a bit more human and said he would see what he could do.

After two days had gone by, I concluded he must have forgotten. I was trying to make up my mind whether it would be wise to try a third guard when my name was called out on one of the seven or eight parades we had during the day and I was escorted to the commandant's office.

The walls of the room were gray, but the fittings were quite luxurious. I noticed a big TV screen, an ornate drinks cabinet, and a plushy daybed on which the commandant could rest when the cares of office overcame him. His chair, too, was an armchair rather than a piece of office furniture, in soft green leather, air-padded by the look of it. His green leather-topped desk had nothing on it but a control panel and a gold pen set. He stared at me as I saluted.

"So you wanted to see me, Anderson. I hope you have a good reason."

"I wondered if you could tell me why I have been sent here, sir."

He laughed with a touch of the bray. "Your

records are kept by your city police. But obviously for the same reason as all the others—extreme misconduct."

"But I haven't done anything."

"No one comes here without a good cause. A police airship delivered you, didn't it?"

"May I tell you how that happened, sir?"

He said, with an air of benevolent contempt, "If you want to. It will make no difference."

I told him my story. At the end, he said, "And what else?"

"Nothing else, sir. That's exactly what happened."

He fixed me with a fat glare. "Don't lie to me, Anderson. I don't like boys who lie. And this is something I can check up on if necessary."

I said quickly, "Then check it, sir. I want you to."

He paused and said, "You were delivered here in the authorized fashion. I'm not going to disturb headquarters on account of a lying boy. Dismiss him, sergeant."

There was something behind the bluster, a touch of uncertainty. He was afraid of his superiors, I guessed. As the guard moved toward me, I said,

"There will be trouble when my father gets back."

"Your father can't change a police order."

"I think he can. He's a councillor."

"Anderson." He looked hard at me. "That Anderson?"

"Yes, sir."

The uncertainty was very plain now; it showed in the twisting of his face, the small movement back into the security of the padded chair. He said, after a moment, "I'll look into it. Now go back to your duties."

Our life in the camp formed a hard and unpleasant routine. First parade was at six in the morning, the last at eight in the evening. Between parades we had marching, drill, physical exercise, and the rest of the time we worked. Most of the work was pointless. We did things like picking up stones and loading them into lorries, which carried them to another part of the island and unloaded them. Sometimes we took them to the end of the breakwater in the old harbor and unloaded them into the sea. Another favored activity involved digging holes and trenches in the ground, which we or other working parties filled in the following day. We were also required to dig holes in the sand on the beaches, but at least did not have to fill them in again; the sea did it for us.

The food was so bad that you needed to be ravenously hungry to eat it—but we were, all the time. Apart from being terrible, there wasn't enough to go round. Fights broke out over crusts of bread, and the guards would watch, laughing, until they tired of the amusement and came in, swinging their batons. Practically without exception they were sadistic bullies.

The dismissal from last parade usually left us too tired to do anything but sleep. Sunyo was an exception to the general rule because he would go out for his meditation, sometimes for as long as an hour. One night, to our surprise, he asked Kelly and me to come with him.

When we were away from the tent, Kelly said, "What's all this? If you were thinking of switching to group meditation, count me out. These days I'm too tired even to daydream about steaks."

Sunyo shook his head. "I found something in the sand today. I want you to help me dig it out."

Kelly groaned. "Not more digging! What is it, anyway?"

"I'm not quite sure, but I've got an idea."

The sun had gone down but it was still light. No one else was about, but the sound of music came from the direction of the guards' houses. Partly intrigued, partly reluctant, we followed Sunyo down the hill, past the ruins of the old town, toward the beach.

We reached the spot where we had been working. The tide was coming in and had already filled some of the holes we had dug that day. Sunyo led us to a point a few yards past the farthest hole and scraped away sand with his fingers. A smooth blue surface showed, and he straightened up.

"Let's get the shovels."

They had been stacked for the night above the tide level.

Kelly said, "Wait a minute."

"What?"

"I don't start digging again without some reason why. You said you had an idea. OK, explain."

"I think it might be a boat," Sunyo said.

"Well?"

"Which we might be able to use to get away from the island."

We stared at him. I said, "To go where? The

nearest city is Cherbourg, and that's at least thirty miles away. You'd never make it. All the nearer coast is Outlands."

Kelly said, "And it's been buried in sand for years, maybe centuries. It'll be rotten."

"It's plastic. Plastic doesn't rot."

Sunyo walked on toward the shovels. We followed him, protesting. I said, "The whole thing's ridiculous. Even if the boat were seaworthy, and by another miracle you managed to get to Cherbourg, what good would that do? They'd only send you back here."

Kelly objected as strongly as I did, but Sunyo paid no attention. I had already noticed that when he had made up his mind about anything he was difficult, if not impossible, to budge. He picked up a shovel and went back to the spot. We watched him digging for a few moments and then Kelly, with an expression of disgust, got another shovel and joined him. Somehow, cursing both Sunyo for his stupid obstinacy and myself for being weak, I found myself following suit.

The sand seemed even damper and heavier than it had been in the afternoon, and I was ready to quit almost as soon as I started. But Sunyo slogged away steadily, and Kelly, though groaning audibly, did the same. Pride kept me digging alongside them.

It was soon clear that Sunyo had been right in his guess. The lines of an upturned hull began to emerge, belonging to a dinghy about nine feet in length. We got down to the gunnels on one side, with the dusk fading into a moonlit night around us and the last of the gulls long since retired. There was no sound but the slap of waves and our own exhausted breathing.

We tried to lever the boat free with our shovels, but it would not budge. Sunyo, without saying anything, started clearing the other side as well, and we reluctantly followed him. We loosened it all round at last and managed to turn it over. I dropped my shovel and lay thankfully on the sand while Kelly and Sunyo examined the boat.

Kelly said grudgingly, "It *looks* sound. But the whole idea is still crazy. As Clive said . . ."

Ignoring him, Sunyo returned to his digging, attacking the sand which had been under the hull.

Kelly demanded, "What are you looking for now? A plastic outboard engine?"

"Oars," Sunyo said, and returned to his task. Kelly and I just watched him; we had had enough. Sunyo at last gave a grunt of satisfaction.

I said, "That doesn't look much like an oar."

He held something up in the dim light; it was a kind of crumpled fabric.

"No," he said. "But a sail. Also of plastic, so that hasn't rotted either."

We stared at him in silence. I didn't know about Kelly, but I was almost too tired to speak. The whole enterprise seemed as pointless as when we had started, if not more so. Sunyo had found his boat, and a sail to go with it. So what?

But Sunyo unmistakably was pleased with himself. He said in quite a cheerful tone, "Just one more thing."

"What's that?"

"Help me carry it. It's fairly light, but I don't think I can manage on my own."

"Are you quite crazy?" Kelly asked. "Carry it where? Back to the tent? Are you proposing to sleep in it?"

"The tide's coming in." Sunyo pointed to the moonlit ripples creeping up to within ten yards of where we stood. "And we need to hide it where the guards won't find it. I marked a good place behind those rocks over there."

Kelly and I looked at one another. Crazy was right, but the whole thing had been crazy. And having come so far, we might as well finish it. We bent down and helped Sunyo lift the boat.

4

NEXT DAY SUNYO WAS IN TROUBLE.

He was disliked by nearly all the guards, probably because they sensed the deep contempt he felt for them as bullies and lackeys, a contempt which even though unspoken showed in his eyes. There was one in particular, though, who detested him and did everything he could to persecute him.

Sunyo's response originally had been silent disgust; he had simply ignored the continual chivvying. Then by accident the guard found a weak spot; he called Sunyo a son of a donkey and saw the

instinctive flash of anger. I never properly under-
stood what it was Sunyo felt about his ancestors—a
remark like that would have meant nothing to
me—but that was where his feelings ran deep, and
that was where he was vulnerable.

Having found the weakness, the guard was quick
to exploit it and took every opportunity to pile on
similar insults. Kelly had seen what was happening
and urged Sunyo not to rise to the jibes, and in fact
Sunyo had made a strenuous effort to ignore them.

Tiredness on this occasion probably made him
edgy—all three of us were feeling the effects of our
extra stint of digging. Fatigue certainly contributed
to the incident which sparked things off. Sunyo was
normally the strongest person on our work team,
but now, lifting a heavy plank into one of the lorries,
he fumbled and dropped his end with a clatter.

The guard, who was only a foot or two away,
laughed. "The descendant of a long line of apes
ought to do better than that!"

I saw Sunyo's mouth tighten, but before I could
do anything to check him, he had slammed into the
guard and knocked him down. Two other guards had
their guns out right away. They forced the rest of us

back while they picked their companion up. A trickle of blood showed at the corner of his mouth. He whispered, "All right, ape boy," and swung his baton.

The beating that followed was bad enough, but there was more to come. The commandant appeared on the next parade and so did Sunyo, his hands pinioned, a guard on either side. His face was badly bruised.

"Obedience," the commandant said. He let the word hang in the air. "Obedience is the road to good citizenship. You are here because you have lost your way, but we are going to set you right."

White clouds scudded across a blue sky. Even for the island, it was windy. Sea birds howled in the distance.

The commandant said, "Obedience as far as you are concerned means obedience to the orders of your guards." He paused. "So what is there to say about a boy who strikes a guard?"

He turned to look at Sunyo. "You will go to the stockade for three days." I was aware of Kelly stiffening beside me. "And then you will make a proper apology to the guard you struck. You will not come out of the stockade until you do."

• • •

The stockade was situated between the parade ground and the guards' houses. It was square in shape, about twelve feet along each side, surrounded by a wooden fence eight or nine feet high. There was a small gate in one side.

Inside there was nothing—no shelter from weather, from sun by day or cold by night. No food was provided. The usual punishment was a day in the stockade, very rarely two days. There had never been a three-day sentence before.

I have left the worst part till last. The floor of the stockade was of concrete which before setting had been formed into ridges and tiny sharp pinnacles. There was discomfort even in standing upright and no way of lying down without hurting yourself.

The guard Sunyo had struck watched him being put inside. He said, "You're going to have a bad time of it, a very bad time. And at the end you are going to crawl at my feet and admit your father was a monkey. I'm looking forward to that."

Sunyo looked at him through blackened eyes. "Never, to scum like you."

The guard laughed. "Carry on talking! It makes the final prospect that much better."

Kelly and I did what we could to make things easier for him. We could not get near him during the day, but at night we were able to sneak out and talk to him through the fence. We saved our bread and tossed it over to him; there was no way of saving the watery stews and gruels which made up the rest of our diet. We also managed to roll a couple of blankets into balls and threw them over, picking them up again early the next morning before the guards were about.

Thirst was not a problem. The hollows in the concrete floor held water, and when, as at present, there was no rain, water was thrown in from a bucket by a guard each day. But to drink, Sunyo had to crouch down like an animal and lap. I could imagine how that made him feel.

The real agony was sleeplessness. By wadding the blankets up in a corner he could manage to doze a little during the night, sitting with his back wedged in the angle, but during the day he had no such

respite. He had either to stand or to accept the tor-
ture of the jagged floor.

The first evening he was low enough in spirits,
the second utterly wretched, the third confused and
rambling.

I said, "At least this is the last night. Tomorrow
afternoon you'll be out."

Sunyo did not speak for a moment. Then: "I
won't crawl to him. Never. . . ."

Kelly said, "It doesn't *mean* anything. And we'll
find a way of getting back at him. The three of us."

I said, "You've got to do it, Sunyo—go through
the motions, anyway."

He whispered again, "Never. I'd rather die."

As we went back to the tent, I said to Kelly,
"He'll feel different when the time comes."

Kelly shook his head. "I wish I could be sure of
that."

"It would be stupid not to do it. And pointless."

"I agree. I'd apologize—crawl if necessary. Then
one night I'd kill him. I think I may do that, anyway.
But Sunyo's different—that pride of his. . . ."

• • •

The desperation of Sunyo's situation was very much in contrast with my own. Since my interview with the commandant I had thought I detected a difference in the attitude of the guards. I came in for less abuse than the others and had an impression I was being given the easier jobs, or at least not landed with the really nasty ones. The feeling was sharpened by an incident on the morning of Sunyo's third day in the stockade.

We were among the ruins of the town, loading granite blocks which we were removing from the crumbling ruin of a church. Most of it had fallen, but part of the belfry remained, raggedly etched against the sky. A guard said:

"We want someone up on top with a pickax. Anderson! No, belay that. Mustn't run risks with the councillor's son. You get up there, Trudillo."

He spoke sarcastically, but it was still significant. I had told no one but Sunyo and Kelly about my father—Sunyo and Kelly and the commandant. Word must have gone out from his office to go easy on me while things were looked into.

It was almost a week since I had been brought

here, four days since I saw the commandant. The order for release could come through at any moment. I could be back in London, in my home, this very day.

I checked my daydreaming with the thought of Sunyo. But at least the end was near; in a few hours he would be out of the stockade.

In the afternoon it was raining. Sunyo's persecutor, with two other guards, opened up the gate and looked through it at Sunyo, who leaned with buckling knees against the fence.

He said, "What a pretty sight. The son of the apes looks more like a drowned rat. Well, time's up. You can come out now."

Sunyo took a few lurching steps toward him. He was soaked through by the rain, which trickled off the waterproof capes of the guards.

"Come on, then," the guard said. "Come on, yellow monkey. Only one little thing to do. Down on your knees and say you're sorry."

Another few steps brought Sunyo in front of him; he stood there, swaying.

"Now," the guard said. "Down."

Sunyo threw himself forward, reaching for the

guard's throat, but it was a pitiable attempt. One hand sent him spinning across the stockade. The guard laughed.

"Still not learned your lesson, monkey? Never mind, there's plenty of time. All the time in the world."

That night Kelly and I went back to the stockade. The rain had stopped and there were fitful indications of moonlight behind the clouds, but it was very dark. We threw our hunks of bread over to Sunyo, but there was not enough light for him to find them.

I was sorry for him, but also angry. I was hungry myself and could have eaten the bread, which now lay somewhere on the wet floor of the stockade. And there was no reason for him to be there, no reason for carrying on this futile business. And the word I had been expecting from the commandant's office had not come yet.

Kelly tossed over the blankets, which Sunyo managed to retrieve. Kelly talked to him, trying to convince him he must give up. He was very weak now and bound to get rapidly weaker. Kelly was very earnest and persuasive. But when he finally stopped, there was only silence from the other side of the fence.

I said bitterly, "He isn't even listening."

"I'm listening," Sunyo said feebly. "But it doesn't do any good. I will not submit to that pig. I can't. The words would choke me."

"Which would you sooner do," I asked, "—choke or starve? Because you're starving to death in there. You can only really defy him by staying alive, and you need strength for that."

"I can't do it."

We both argued with him, but with no success. We left him in the end and set off back toward the tent. The clouds were breaking up, showing the light of a three-quarter moon.

Kelly said suddenly, "Only one thing for it."

"What?"

"We've got to get him out."

I laughed. "Sure. That's the answer."

"I mean it. He'll die sooner than give in. I'm certain of it."

"So what do you suggest? Do we go along to the guards' houses and ask for the key to the stockade, then come back and open up?"

"Blankets," Kelly said. "We can tie them together in a rope and haul him out."

I was tired as well as hungry and looking forward to wrapping myself up in the one blanket I had left. I said, "And if we get him out, what happens? He'll still be on the island. He'll have to give himself up eventually. They'll know who helped him, so all it means is that when he's put back in the stockade, he finds us waiting for him."

"He doesn't have to be on the island." I looked at him. "There's the boat."

"You said yourself that was ridiculous."

"I thought so then. Things have changed. He'll die in there if we don't get him away."

"He'd die in the boat. We don't even know if it's seaworthy. And there's no means of navigating. Anyway, where do you wind up? If it's a city, you get brought back here. If it's the Outlands, you get killed by savages."

Kelly said, "Look, all I'm asking is for you to help me with the stockade part. You don't have to come in the boat."

"The whole thing's mad." Kelly did not reply; we were almost at the tent. "All right, I'll help you."

. . .

We went in quietly and picked up the other two blankets. Everyone seemed to be asleep; at least, no one asked us what we were doing. The clouds were continuing to clear, and we could see our way back to the stockade reasonably well.

Kelly told Sunyo what he proposed. Sunyo tried to argue, saying there was no reason why anyone else should get involved, but he was too weak and miserable to put up much opposition. Kelly knotted our two blankets together and threw them across the top of the fence, and Sunyo, though more slowly, tied his two blankets onto the end.

But at the next stage he failed. The idea was that while Kelly and I held on, Sunyo would swarm up the blanket rope and so get out. He did make an attempt—we could hear him scrabbling against the inside of the fence—but had to give up.

He said, "It's no good. No strength in my arms. You go back. Thank you for trying, but it's no use."

I was prepared to agree, but Kelly said, "Clive, make a back. I'm going in."

He climbed on my shoulders, reached for the top of the fence, and hauled himself up. He gave a grunt of pain as a spike of wood dug into him, then dropped inside. I heard his whispered instructions to Sunyo.

"Take an end and get up on my back. I'll crouch down." He called through to me, "Clive, heave on your end when I say the word."

The first time Sunyo slipped down before the word could be given, and there was another exclamation from Kelly as he fell over along with him. But he got Sunyo in position again and pushed him up.

"OK, Clive. Now!"

I pulled hard on my end. The blanket was taut across the top of the fence, and there was the full weight of Sunyo on it as well. I didn't think I could budge him. But as I sweated and strained, Kelly managed to get his hands under Sunyo's feet and thrust him higher. I pulled again, and suddenly the tension slackened. A moment later I saw in the moonlight the dim figure of Sunyo on top of the fence. He fell rather than jumped, landing beside me.

All that remained was to get Kelly out. He pulled himself up by means of the blanket and crashed heavily down on our side. Both he and Sunyo seemed to have made a lot of noise, but fortunately loud music was coming from the direction of the guards' houses.

It still seemed a good idea to get out of the area as quickly as possible.

Sunyo was very weak, and we had to stop several times on the way to the beach to let him rest. When we got there, he collapsed on the sand and Kelly and I went to the place behind the rocks where we had left the boat. I had half a hope that the guards might have found it and taken it away; the sea, though calm in the moonlight, looked horribly wide and unwelcoming.

But we found the boat. Kelly said, "I'll take this end. OK to lift?"

I said, "Wait a minute."

"What's that?"

"I've been thinking. Those caves on the far side of the island . . . we could hide him there."

"Hopeless," Kelly said. "They'd find him in a few hours with a search party. Even if they didn't, how long do you think it could last? Days at the most, then back to the stockade. Forget it."

"Days might be enough. It won't be long before my father gets me out of here. Tomorrow maybe. He might be able to do something."

"For you, yes. I don't doubt that. But not for Sunyo. This place is under the International Police.

Your father may be a councillor in London, but he has no authority in Kyoto."

I could not dispute that. I racked my brain to find another argument which would persuade him to drop this harebrained scheme.

Kelly said, "You've been a great help, Clive. I mean it. I couldn't have got him out of the stockade by myself. Just help me get the boat down now, and that's enough. Take your two blankets back to the tent, and there'll be no way of tying you in with us being missing. Don't worry—we'll make it."

"Make it where? To the Outlands?"

"As far as we're concerned, the Outlands are better than staying here. I promise you."

So I helped him carry the boat down. In addition to the plastic sails and ropes there was a collapsible mast. It had metal trimmings which had rusted to nothing, but the mast itself seemed in fair shape. I helped Kelly fit it into its socket and rig the sails after a fashion.

"There's not much wind," I said.

Kelly was wrestling with the boom. "Not much. But enough."

"And what there is is onshore."

"Yes, but the tide's making northwest. We'll get clear, all right."

I shrugged. Argument was plainly useless.

Kelly said, "If we can float her and you can lend a hand with Sunyo . . ."

We wrestled the boat over the sand and into the water. There was still a chance the hull would prove not to be watertight, and even Kelly could scarcely propose setting off in a vessel that was leaking. He clambered in while I held on.

"How is it?"

"Sound as a bell." A wave splashed in, halfway up my thighs. "I'll hang on now while you get Sunyo."

Sunyo did not reply when I first spoke to him, and I thought he was asleep or had fainted. But he roused himself and sat up slowly and painfully. In the moonlight he looked terrible.

I said, "Lean on me."

He shook his head. "I can walk."

He did it, with an immense effort but unaided. I remembered he had had nothing to eat for three days except a couple of crusts of bread and tonight not even that. He waded into the sea and staggered as a small wave hit him, but recovered.

He needed help, though, to get into the boat. Somehow Kelly and I hauled him over the side, with the dinghy rocking violently and threatening to turn over. Kelly got in after him. He said, "Thanks for everything, Clive."

"I still think . . ."

"I know you do." His teeth gleamed in moonlight as he grinned. "And you could be right. But it looks different from where we're standing. Best of luck. I hope your release comes through soon."

"Best of luck to you. You need it more than I do."

"Sure. If you can contribute just one little push to get us moving . . ."

I waded forward, pushing the dinghy out. The beach shelved under my feet. A receding wave tugged at the boat, pulling it from me. That was when instead of pushing I gripped the gunnel and heaved myself on board. The dinghy rocked and shipped water but righted itself.

Kelly asked, in genuine surprise, "What do you think you're up to?"

"It looks as though I'm coming with you." I looked at the shore behind us. "Don't ask me why, because I don't know."

5

I ASKED MYSELF THE QUESTION AGAIN AS THE dinghy drifted out on the tide and the distance from shore steadily increased, and the only answer was that I was an idiot. I did not flatter myself that I was doing Kelly and Sunyo any good by going with them; if anything, the reverse was true. The biggest danger to the boat was the risk of swamping, and the addition of a third person would only increase that.

I had climbed aboard on impulse, and the impulse was short-lived. It was replaced by another: to dive in and swim ashore while I still could. I think I might have done so, except that Sunyo groaned faintly and Kelly said, "Clive, see if you can help him get comfortable while I deal with this sail."

I did what I could with the help of Kelly's blankets. My own two were on the beach where I had left them. I should have had the sense to bring them, but, more to the point, I should have had the sense to swim back and pick them up and head for the tent. Inside ten minutes I could have been wrapped up and asleep on solid ground, instead of rocking in this cockleshell on a very large and very wet sea.

When I looked toward shore again, it was more than a hundred yards away, not an easy swim against what was plainly a strong tide. The island was taking on shape in the moonlight, the long line of beach curving out and the higher ground to the south coming in view. I looked the other way and there was nothing but sea, featureless except for the broad flickering path cast by the moon.

I said to Kelly, "Is there any particular destination in mind, or do we just drift?"

He pointed at the moon. "As long as that's on our left, we're heading roughly east. The coast of France is almost due east."

But nine miles away, I remembered. I said, "What sort of speed do you think we're making?"

Kelly shook his head. "No idea."

He sounded very cheerful, a good deal more cheerful than I felt. Much as I had hated life in the camp, I was beginning to see certain advantages to it—things like food and solid ground. And the possibility that at any moment a guard might yell, "Anderson, report to the commandant's office!" Maybe on first parade tomorrow . . . but it would do me no good now.

The island dwindled, fading into the moonlit haze of sea and sky. I became conscious of the emptiness of my stomach. It was six hours or more since supper, which had been only watery stew since we had saved our bread for Sunyo.

I thought of something else and said to Kelly, "Water. . . ."

"Yes." He laughed. "You don't realize how much of it there is in the sea."

"Drinking water. We haven't got any."

After a pause, he said, "Yes. That was a bit stupid. I didn't think."

I looked at the vague, distant smudge of the island.

"Do you think we ought to go back and get some?"

"No chance. It's not just the tide—what wind there is would be against us."

We were silent again. Kelly said, "Less than ten miles to France. If it takes all night we won't be too bad. We're not going to die of thirst before morning."

It was meant to be cheerful, and I supposed I ought to have been able to say something cheerful back, but I could not think of anything. Sunyo lay wrapped in blankets, and Kelly and I sat upright, watching the sea in silence.

It must have been half an hour later that I said, "The moon."

It was moving very slowly across the sky, from its station on our left hand to a position dead ahead. That was the impression. The reality was that the boat was swinging north in a current far stronger than the gentle following wind.

Kelly said, "Yes, I've seen it." He sounded grimmer. "The tide must run really fierce between the island and the French coast."

"What happens now?"

"It will take us north into the main part of the English Channel. It should ease after that. We might find enough wind to take us back to France."

"And if we don't get the wind?"

"Well, there's land to the north as well, isn't there? The south coast of England."

"Not nine miles away, though. More like seventy."

"Sure. We won't be in for breakfast."

"And the tide may not take us north. It could take us west, into the ocean."

"You're a great little ray of sunshine." The grimness had turned angry. "You got any other comforting speculations to offer?"

"When I told you how mad the scheme was," I said, "you wouldn't listen. And apart from that, you just forgot to bring any drinking water along. You've been doing very well so far."

"Shut up," Kelly said. "We didn't ask you to come, Mr. Councillor's son. Swim back, and welcome. If you don't feel like doing that, shut up."

He was angry and afraid, as I was too. I thought of several cutting things but did not say them. My mouth felt dry. Suddenly, despite the coolness of the night, I was very thirsty.

• • •

The weather deteriorated. It was first apparent in a freshening of the wind and increased choppiness of the waves. It freshened from the wrong quarter, from the southeast. Our chances of getting to France were diminishing rapidly.

Sunyo woke up in order to be sick, or rather to retch from an empty stomach. It was not long before Kelly followed suit, as the sea grew rougher and the dinghy tossed on it like a cork. I held out longer but succumbed at last. Clouds crossed the moon—in wisps at first, then thicker till it was completely obscured. I could scarcely see the sea but could hear it well enough, in wind and wave, and feel it when a wave slapped over the gunnels and drenched me through.

After a very long time there was light in the east. It slowly brightened, but the sky stayed gray and cloud-covered, and the sea was gray all round us. I strained my eyes for a sight of land, but there was nothing, not even a sea bird to break the heaving monotony of the waste of water.

The others were also awake and looking about them. Kelly asked Sunyo how he felt, and he said he was all right. Surprisingly, he did look a little better.

Kelly said, "Not much for breakfast, I'm afraid."

His grin included me, and I willingly took the olive branch. I said, "I was thinking of eggs and bacon. Three eggs, no—four. And half a dozen rashers. With a very big cup of coffee. Creamy coffee."

"Ham and eggs for me," Kelly said. "Buckwheat cakes and honey. And fresh orange juice. A lot of fresh orange juice."

The thought made me realize how thirsty I was. I did not feel like going on with that particular game, and neither, it seemed, did Kelly. We stared glumly at the surrounding sea. Sunyo was staring at it, too. He spoke, more to himself than anyone else, and I thought I'd misheard him. I asked, "What was that?"

"It's beautiful."

"Beautiful?" I had heard him right. "What is?"

"The two colors of gray: the sky and the sea. They're almost the same, and yet there is a contrast. My father had a picture in which there was an effect something like that. It was a scroll which you held in one hand and unrolled with the other, showing a panorama of landscape starting high in the mountains and going down to the sea. That was where the two grays were."

Incredible, I thought, that he could talk about pictures in a situation like this. Though it could be an advantage. Anything was which took our minds off the spot we were in. As though thinking along the same lines, Kelly started talking about his home, but in connection with dogs, not pictures—his father bred King Charles spaniels as a hobby. I contributed our tropical fish tank, which took up one wall of the sitting room.

Sunyo remained silent, meditating maybe, but Kelly and I went on trying to reminisce ourselves out of this watery wilderness. He spoke of the race course they had in Jacksonville, something London could not boast. I countered it by describing the stretch of river just inside the wall which had been designed as a swimming center, with individual pools on the north bank and the temperature of the whole river raised more than ten degrees by heating elements on the riverbed. Londoners were proud of the amount of energy they could afford to spend in that way.

"Kind of a waste, isn't it?" Kelly said. "I mean, heating up a whole river."

"You waste land on a race course. All our public land is parks."

I spoke a bit sharply, and he replied in the same tone. "Our parks are as good as any you have in London, with poinsettias and jacaranda and oranges growing out in the open. You can walk through a Jacksonville park and pick oranges off the trees and eat them."

The image was powerful and made my throat seem more parched than ever. I said dispiritedly, "Jacksonville or London—what's the difference? We're a long way from either."

Time dragged by. The cloud cover remained unbroken, a heavy pall stretching from skyline to dim skyline. A sight of the sun, even a patch of brightness, would have given us some idea of the direction in which we were drifting, but in this featureless seascape we could equally be heading north toward England or south back to France. Also, and I began to fear it more and more, we could be on course for nothing but the immense emptiness of the western ocean. Kelly's Florida lay that way, but I doubted if he would have any enthusiasm for trying to get home by such a route.

Sunyo said little. Kelly and I had spells of talking,

more often wrangling, intermingled with periods of gloomy silence. Apart from hunger and thirst, there was tiredness; despite the discomfort, I found myself dozing off, waking with a start to the wretchedness of my surroundings. As the day wore on, the gray of sky deepened. Night fell and it turned black, pitch black, with no trace of moonlight.

I slept and woke and slept again. I had disjointed dreams that were more like nightmares, but there was one that was different. I was in my speedboat on the river, and Miranda was there, too. I started telling her what had happened since I saw her—about being sent to the island and escaping by boat—and it was all in the past and exciting to talk about. She listened, with her blond hair tossed over one shoulder. I was pleased to have her to myself, then realized, as one does in a dream, that this wasn't true because Gary was there as well. I told him what I thought of him, and since that did not seem to be enough, I also hit him. We flailed at each other on the deck of the speedboat, and the next moment I was in the water.

I woke up feeling wetness and thought the dream had become reality. But the wetness was of stinging drops on my face and hands. I realized it was raining.

I called to the others and they answered. After that, I was too concerned with trying to catch the rain. I cupped my hands against my cheeks, collecting rain drops and licking them up. No orange juice could have tasted so good.

The rain lasted about half an hour, long enough to take the edge off our thirst but not to quench it. The wind had risen with the rain, and more and more waves were slopping over the gunnels. Water pooled round my feet; not much yet, but it would increase. The threat of swamping began to loom again.

It would not have been so bad if we had had something to bail with. But there were too many ifs. If we had brought a supply of drinking water, if we had raided the cook house for food, if Kelly had taken my advice to hide Sunyo in a cave rather than embark on this crack-brained voyage. . . . Indignation rose once more, but I reminded myself of another if. I had clambered on board of my own volition; I could not blame anyone else for that.

We tried to bail out water with our hands, though with no apparent effect. I felt sick and cold—the blankets lay soaked in the well of the boat—and tired to the point of being dazed. The night seemed interminable, the battering of wind and waves unending. At least things could scarcely get worse, I thought, when with a sharp cracking sound the mast broke off near its foot and fell to one side, taking the furled sail with it.

The mast dipped into the water and dragged the boat over. We were shipping seas fast and had no option but to get rid of it, so we struggled to untie and loose the ropes. At last we had the mast free and could cast it adrift. We were safe from immediate capsizing, but the water was round our ankles. We set to work bailing again furiously.

Gradually the sky lightened into the dawn of our second day at sea, still with no sight of land anywhere. I looked at Sunyo, huddled in the stern, and Kelly, lying in several inches of water in the well. They didn't make a pretty sight, but I knew I must look no better. I saw, too, the broken stump of the mast. Even if land had been in sight, how could we get to it with neither sail nor oars? We were at the mercy of wind and tide.

There could be only one end: if not death by

drowning, then by exhaustion or thirst. The former would be kinder; our strenuous bailing had only preserved us for a longer-lasting misery. This morning the wind had dropped and the sea was less rough, churning in a long swell.

None of us felt much like talking. My own mind was a morass of hopelessness lit by flashes of resentment—against Sunyo for hitting the guard, against Kelly for insisting on this lunatic scheme, against the commandant, the London police, Gary—even against my father for being away on holiday. None of this did me any good; it only made me more miserable. But I couldn't help it.

At least I no longer wrangled with Kelly; I think we were both too deadbeat. Minutes, hours drifted by, meaningless in the blankness of sea and sky. I suppose it was roughly in the middle of the day that Sunyo spoke.

"Listen."

I did so apathetically and heard the slap of waves against the side of the boat, all too familiar.

Kelly said, "Listen to what?"

"That noise," Sunyo said. "It sounds like an airship engine."

I listened then. At first I could still hear only the waves. It was Kelly who said, with a lift in his voice, "I think you're right!"

I heard it myself almost immediately: a tiny distant drone in the sky. We roused ourselves, our eyes desperately searching. Sunyo was also the first to spot it and point it out: a black speck against the cloud.

It was so small, and the sky was so big, as was, I realized, the sea in which this little dinghy rocked. Although we could see the airship, that did not mean it was coming anywhere near us. I watched in an agony of anxiety. The speck did not seem to be moving, and I said so.

"That's a good sign," Kelly said. "If it were moving, it would be crossing our field of vision. It must be coming toward us. It looks bigger."

Was it? With a leap of joy I realized he was right; it was getting bigger. And I could hear the hum of the motor more clearly.

I stood up, frantically waving. Kelly shouted, "Careful, you fool, you'll capsize us," but I was too happy to mind it.

Sunyo said, more reasonably, "It is too far off

still. No one could see us. But I think it is on course for us, in a direct line almost."

We watched the airship approaching, and I had time to think about what would happen after we were picked up. Back to the island, of course, and perhaps back to the stockade for Sunyo. No, that was certain, and very likely Kelly with him. But first there would be food and drink, baths, sleep in soft beds. And maybe what we had been through had taught Sunyo to be less pigheaded.

As for me, I was sure that by now the order for my release must have come through. I even had a crazy notion that my father might be in the airship, directing a search for us. That was absurd, I knew, but at least we were going to be rescued. Nothing else mattered.

The airship, a white civil aircraft, came steadily on, flying at no more than two hundred feet above the sea. Its flight path was taking it just a little to the left of us, and we could see the windows of the dining cabin, with small figures at the tables. We were all standing up and waving now, with the dinghy rocking perilously beneath us.

We shouted as well as waved, even though we

knew sound could not carry to the sealed cabins. But they must see us! We could see them so clearly. A waiter was bending over one table, pouring out wine. It was impossible that we could be missed. Even when the airship had passed overhead, I was sure of that. Someone must see us, and the airship would turn back again.

Then Sunyo said in a cold, dry voice, "They've not seen us. And they won't now."

He sat down heavily, and Kelly did the same. I stood and gazed at the airship, diminishing in size with the passing moments. The sound of the motor faded and was lost in the monotonous slap of waves. I sat down myself and huddled in the stern.

The rest of the day was very bad. Before we saw the airship, we had begun to be resigned to the prospect of dying. Hope had sharpened our will to live, and its loss tormented us. Our ears were continually pricked for the sound of an engine; our eyes futilely searched the gray above for a sight of movement. But it was pointless, and we knew it. If an airship passing so closely overhead had not seen us, what chance was there of any other doing so? Yet we went on watching compulsively, torturing ourselves with impossible hopes.

In a way it was a relief when dusk put an end to it. I looked out as the horizon drew in and wondered what our chances were of surviving the night. The wind seemed to be increasing again. We had summoned up reserves of strength in shouting and waving to the airship, but I doubted if any remained. I could not see us bailing out with our hands in another squall. Drowning, anyway, would be better than lingering on.

Kelly and Sunyo had changed places, and Sunyo was now lying in the water at the bottom of the boat. He was sleeping, and I thought that Kelly, slumped in the bow, was asleep also. But he said something in a low voice which I did not catch.

After a moment he spoke again, more clearly. "Over there. . . ."

I felt I ought to say something but was almost too tired to utter. I mumbled, "What?"

"Could it be land?"

He was talking in his sleep, I thought, or maybe delirious. There was nothing but sea.

He said, "Dead ahead. Behind you, that is. Could it be?"

I turned, awkwardly. More sea stretched interminably away until it merged into the deepening murk of sky. I felt a small flash of anger at him, but was too weak to feel anything strongly.

I was turning back in silence when Kelly said in a louder voice, "I think it is land!"

Was that a darker line between the two grays? I thought I saw it, lost it, saw it again. It was tantalizingly uncertain. Sunyo had better vision than either Kelly or I, and I leaned forward and put out a hand to wake him, but Kelly stopped me.

"Don't. No point in raising false hopes. Even if it is land, what can we do about it? It must be a couple of miles away, and I doubt if any of us has the strength to swim a couple of yards."

I saw the point, and we sat and watched in silence. It was certainly land, a coast that stretched away into darkness, and after a time there could be no doubt that the tide was taking us in. But slowly, slowly, and I was all too conscious that tides could change. In that case we would drift back into the night that was rapidly closing down, a night that must be final.

Declining visibility and the narrowing distance contended with one another. The coast ahead was only a blur, but the blur grew nearer. We wakened Sunyo at last, and for a moment he, too, stared unbelievingly. He started trying to paddle with an arm over the side of the boat, and Kelly and I did the same. We were so feeble that our hands could do little more than brush the surface, but we had the illusion of doing something.

Under an almost black sky we drifted in toward a black shore. I heard a grating sound, and felt the weird sensation of something solid underneath us. We had reached land.

6

I SCRAMBLED OVER THE SIDE INTO THE WATER. Stones rolled under my feet. I was submerged to the waist and a wave surged up into my face, making me gasp and almost making me lose my hold on the boat. I saw Sunyo try to rise and fall back.

I asked Kelly, "Do you think he can get out? Or can you heave him over to me?"

Sunyo said weakly, "I'm all right."

He needed help all the same. Between us we got him into the water, and I supported him as we staggered up toward the beach. The sea grew shallower, and suddenly I was on dry land. That was when, without the buoyancy of the water, weakness really hit me. I staggered another step or two and collapsed. Sunyo managed to stay upright a moment longer; then he went down as well.

Behind us, Kelly was trying to drag the boat up out of the water. He called for help, and somehow I summoned the strength to go back to him. We hauled on either side of the bow, pulling the boat up onto the shingle. It came a little way and stuck. Kelly urged me to pull again, and I made another effort with my aching arms.

With a wrench and a screech of stones the boat moved perhaps a foot and stopped.

I said, "That's it."

"We've got to get it higher."

"It's high enough." I didn't feel I had the strength to pull a kitten across a polished floor. "I'm going to see to Sunyo."

In the darkness I almost fell over him. I started lifting him, but he got up by himself. We tottered together over the scrunching pebbles, and I wasn't sure who was helping whom. Somehow we made it to a point where our progress was barred by a low escarpment, no more than knee high. I felt sand, and tufted grass growing along the top. I heaved myself up, and Sunyo flopped beside me. Kelly, reeling along behind, came up with us a few seconds later.

We lay in utter exhaustion. I felt wide awake in mind but physically deadbeat to the point of help-lessness. I considered the possibility of lifting a hand from the sand on which it lay, but the effort would have been altogether too much. I was fully aware of my surroundings, though, and in particular of the wonderful absence of movement, the solid-ness of the earth beneath me. I could hear the mur-mur and growl of the sea as it rolled pebbles up and down the beach. Let it roll them—incredibly, we were free of its clutches.

Kelly said, "The boat. . . ."

"What about the boat?"

"We ought to have another shot at getting it out."

I heard him struggle to his feet, looked up at his dim figure, and marveled at the feat. I thought again of lifting my hand but did not try. Kelly bent down and tugged at me.

"Come on, Clive."

I would have been angry if I had had strength for

it. And suddenly I was tired in mind as well as body, with sleep rolling in on me like a wave—but dry and comforting, not wet and violent.

I said, yawning, "Boat's all right. Stop worrying."

He said something else, but I wasn't interested. I had a vague impression of Kelly himself lying down before the wave blanked me out.

When I woke there was the light of dawn in the sky, my limbs were aching, and my mouth and throat were dry. I tried to swallow and couldn't. Thirst seemed to have spread through every inch of my body; quenching it was all I could think about. Sunyo and Kelly were sprawled asleep beside me and the sea rumbled behind us. I did not wake them but managed to stand and take a few steps forward. It was dark still, but I saw the shapes of trees in the distance and hobbled in that direction.

Between the top of the beach and the line of forest lay about fifty yards of small sandy dunes, thinly sprinkled with grass. The dragging sand made my feet leaden, but the thought of water kept me going. I could see the trees more clearly, their tops moving in a light dawn wind; in this light they were gray rather than green. A single bird gave a hoarse, shrieking cry. Apart from that, there was no sound but the sigh of the wind, the more distant roar of the sea, and the scuffing of my feet in the sand.

Soon I was near enough to pick out individual trees, but I was aware of the dark unknown behind them. I heard a noise ahead—a sharp, cracking sound like someone breaking a stick. Or something. I stopped and, as I did so, heard, in a stillness as the wind dropped, something else—a low continuous gurgling, the ripple of running water. I plunged recklessly forward into the forest.

It had sounded misleadingly near. I hunted among the trees, with bushes tearing my clothes. I thought I had lost it; then it was quite loud. The floor of the forest rose and dipped and the stream was in front of me, running between high banks, narrow but swift.

I half scrambled, half fell toward it and put my face into the water, gulping like an animal and afterward cupping my hands to drink deeply from them. Gradually the fierce ache of thirst grew less. I drank again, but more slowly, and rubbed water into my face with my fingers. Then I got up, climbed the bank, and set off to find the others.

Although I thought I had come out of the wood not far from where I had entered it, I could see no sign of Kelly and Sunyo. The sky was lighter and I could see the ridge plainly, but there was nothing there but sand and grass. Could I possibly have confused my direction so completely, or had they perhaps seen and followed me? I was turning back toward the wood when I heard faint voices from the opposite direction. They must be on the beach.

I called and waved from the escarpment and they came toward me across the shingle. Sunyo looked bad in the harsh morning light, his skin very yellow and drawn tight over the bones of his face. Kelly looked strange, too, but I soon realized it was from anger rather than illness.

He said in a hard whisper, "Do you have to shout like that? Don't you understand these are the Outlands? Do you want a horde of savages whooping round us?"

"The beach is deserted," I said. "You can see for miles. There's nothing the other way either, except empty forest. What were you doing on the beach, anyway?"

"Looking for the boat. We didn't find it. If you'd been willing to make an extra bit of effort last night, we could have got it up. As it is, the tide's taken it. It's probably halfway to France by now."

"What difference does it make?"

"The difference between being stuck in this god-forsaken hole and perhaps finding our way along the coast to somewhere more promising. That's all."

"A boat," I said, "—without oars, with a broken mast and no sail."

"We could have made oars."

I laughed. "Using what?"

"Or rigged a jury mast and some kind of sail—with our shirts, maybe."

"You have to be crazy."

I was angry enough to hit him but had a horrible suspicion that if I tried to swing I might fall over.

Sunyo said, "Forget it. The boat's gone and there's no point in arguing about it. We have other things to think of—food and water in the first place."

His calmness cooled our tempers. Kelly shrugged.

I said, "The water problem's solved, at least. I found a stream, just inside the wood."

Kelly's face cleared completely. He said, "OK, Macduff. Lead on."

I led the way up over the escarpment and across the dunes to the forest. I could see it more clearly now and get some idea of its density and vastness. There was high ground far off, as thickly wooded as that which confronted us.

Viewing it without the urgency of thirst, I had a quick and terrifying understanding of where we were and what all this was. The Outlands. There was no telling what might lie among the dark tangle behind the gently waving screen of leaves. I thought of the wild beasts of the servants' stories. A sound in the distance rose and fell: the wind in the trees or the howl of a wolf? I stopped abruptly.

Kelly said, "What's up? You forgotten the way?"

Or savages calling to one another—perhaps already aware of us and moving forward in a closing circle for the attack? Sunyo was looking at me, too.

I took a grip on myself and said, "I wasn't sure for a moment. It's over there."

We pushed through the undergrowth into the wood and found the stream, and they drank their fill. I drank again myself, even though I wasn't thirsty.

When we stood up at last, Kelly said, "That's a lot better. All we need now is food. Any sign of coconuts or breadfruit trees?"

The trees surrounding us seemed to bear nothing but leaves, though those in abundance. I did not recognize any of them; they were certainly not the planes and ornamental cherries and evergreens that grew decorously in rows in London parks. There was nothing in the least decorous about these trees. They grew in a wild confusion and competition, some strong and broad-trunked, others thin and sickly and overshadowed. It all looked mixed up and pointless and depressing.

Sunyo said, "There's nothing here. We'd better go on."

Kelly nodded. "Follow the stream."

"I don't agree," I said. "I think we ought to get back in the open and go along the coast."

"What's the point?" Kelly asked. "We know what there is there—nothing but sand and shingle and seawater."

"We might catch fish."

"With what? And how do we cook them?"

"At least we'd be able to see where we were going. You can't see more than a couple of feet ahead of you in this jungle."

That was what I found unnerving: not being able to see, coupled with the feeling that something might at any moment emerge from the next bush.

Kelly said, "Well, I'm for following the stream. It must lead us somewhere—maybe to a river."

I said stubbornly, "It's more likely to lead back to the sea; in which case we've wasted time and effort and are no better off. I vote for the beach."

Kelly looked from me to Sunyo, who said, "I think Kelly's right. And it means staying close to fresh water. That might be important later on."

Kelly said, "OK, Clive?"

I thought of arguing but was too tired and hungry and fed up. I remembered again that but for him I would probably now be at home, perhaps watching early-morning TV, with Bobby bringing me my breakfast tray. I shrugged.

"Just as you like."

• • •

So we followed the course of the stream, though from time to time we had to leave it and detour around patches of dense undergrowth. At the beginning I expected that we would fairly soon come out to the sea—the stream could not have been more than a hundred yards from the beach at the point where I had found it—and that I would have the satisfaction of seeing my point proved. But we remained in the forest, progressing, as the growing light in the sky in front of us showed, steadily toward the east.

No one said much. As we went on, I began to think more clearly and logically about our position. The coast onto which we had drifted ran more or less east-west. Unless it was some freak of geography, that made it overwhelmingly probable that we were on the south coast of England. There were three cities situated on that coast: Plymouth, Southampton, and Dover. The likelihood was that Southampton was the nearest and also that we were heading roughly in that direction.

My spirits improved when I had worked this out. In a few hours—at any moment, even—the trees might thin to give a view of cleared land and the city's wall in the distance. Then all I had to do was go to the gate and call the guard. Mr. Sherrin would pick me up, and I could visiphone my father; he must surely be back in London by now. I wondered if there would be a chance of seeing Miranda before I caught the airship back.

As for Kelly and Sunyo, presumably they would have to return to the island. But I was sure my father would be able to do something to help them, even if he could not get them released right away. And being sent back to the island was better than wandering, lost and starving, through the Outlands.

We had seen nothing so far but trees and plants, but I was not much reassured by that. And the plants themselves were so alien. I thought of those in the city parks, bearing big colorful blooms, each with its name-tag. Flowers grew here, beside the brook, but the blossoms were small and unobtrusive. They were dull. The Outlands were dull altogether—dull and unfriendly and unsettling.

Kelly stopped by a bush hung with blue berries. He said, "They look like huckleberries."

"Huckleberries?"

"I saw them in a park in Boston, when I stayed

with my aunt. They're OK to eat. Do you know if huckleberries grow in England?"

I shook my head. "Not in London, anyway. I wouldn't try them if I were you."

Kelly did not answer but plucked a berry and put it in his mouth. He made a wry face and spat it out again.

"No, thanks. I'm not that hungry." He stared at the stream, here rushing fiercely over tumbled stones. "You think there could be fish in there?"

"I've not seen any. I should think it's too shallow. Even if there were and we could catch them, as you said, we've no way of cooking them."

"I could eat mine raw." He grinned at Sunyo. "Don't you eat raw fish in Japan?"

"Specially prepared and with sauces. But I agree with you. I could do without the sauces."

The patch of light marking the presence of the sun was still ahead and fairly high now. The cloud cover seemed to be thinning; occasionally we had a glimpse of a bright disk. It was gradually growing warmer, too; our wet shirts dried on our backs. We were very tired, and hunger nagged more sharply with the passing hours. Had I not read some story of the Dark Ages, in which people had nibbled bark from the trees? It was no longer incredible.

There had been occasional clearings, mostly where rocky outcrops kept down the vegetation, and I assumed the new one we reached was of the same kind. But there were differences. For one thing it was bigger in extent, perhaps fifty yards across, and it also had a regular, almost squared-off look. But I was more immediately concerned with the sight of the animals which rushed from it through the bushes only a yard or two from where we stood. They were as big as dogs but fatter, with gray hairy skins and stubby legs, on which they moved with a surprising turn of speed. They made grunting noises as they went, and I recognized them from pictures. They were pigs.

Wild pigs, that would be, and they looked frightening, showing the gleam of ferocious white tusks. I halted right away, but Kelly went forward.

He said, "Boy, look at this! Breakfast at last."

For a moment I thought he was talking about the pigs and that he had gone crazy. I had absolutely no intention of tackling that lot—there had been more than half a dozen, one quite enormous—and in any case they had disappeared into the wood. But he was looking into the clearing, and I saw another way in which it was different.

The clearing had been planted out in lines. I saw rows of cabbages, where it looked as though the pigs had been rooting, furrows topped with tangled green plants bearing tiny white and purple flowers, and other lines of plants supported by sticks. There were long green beans hanging from some and ripe tomatoes from others.

It was a vegetable patch. Savages must have planted it, though it was a bit of a shock to realize that savages could be intelligent enough to make gardens. Then where were they? There was no sign of life, but they must live somewhere in the neighborhood. I was going to say something about that, but Kelly was already on his way toward the tomato plants. He plucked a tomato and dug his teeth into it.

"Great! Really great."

Sunyo said, "We ought to be cautious."

I agreed, but the sight of Kelly eating was too much for me, and I followed him and picked one myself. The juice was sweet and good. I wolfed the tomato and started on another. Sunyo had joined in by now, and all three of us had our attentions fixed no more than inches in front of us—on the next tomato. But perhaps Sunyo was less gluttonous than Kelly and I or more wary by nature. He said in a quiet voice, "We're being watched."

His head flicked slightly toward a point on our right. Something moved in the bushes. I saw a man's figure, then another. Kelly had seen them, too. I drew my hand back from the tomato I was reaching for, and Kelly said, "Savages. Run for it—in the opposite direction. When I say go."

He gave the word, and we took to our heels. Figures burst from the bushes a long way behind us. I tried to run faster. Then more figures appeared, coming from the bushes directly in front. There were half a dozen of them, wearing nothing but short breeches made out of coarse cloth and sandals on their feet. But they were carrying nasty-looking clubs and looked more than ready to use them. We stopped, and before we had time to think again, the rest were up with us.

One of them spoke. I could not make out what he said except that it was threatening. Kelly moved slightly, and several clubs were raised by strongly muscled arms.

Sunyo said, "Don't resist. I don't think they are going to kill us."

I wondered what made him think that and hoped he was right; they looked murderous to me. But resistance, in any case, would obviously be futile. Sunyo put his hand up in a gesture of surrender, and Kelly and I copied him.

The savage spoke again. His tone didn't sound any more pleasant than before, but the clubs were dropped.

The village, which was not far away, consisted of primitive wooden huts. We saw women and children there as well as men but did not have much chance to study them. We were pushed into one of the huts, and I fell sprawling on a floor of beaten earth.

On the way the savages had been talking to one another, and I had begun to pick out words here and there. It was a dialect English, such as the servants used among themselves, but coarser and more difficult to understand. I managed, though, to get the drift of their talk. It seemed the wild pigs were in the habit of raiding the vegetable patch and that the savages in turn used it as bait for providing themselves with supplies of fresh pork. The man who had been on duty guarding the patch had seen the arrival of the pigs and gone back to the village to round up a hunting party. But we had surprised the pigs first, and the savages had arrived to find us eating their crops instead. It was difficult to tell whether they were more angry over that or over losing a promising haul of meat. What was certain was that they were not at all pleased.

If anything was said of their intentions concerning us, I missed it, and so did Kelly and Sunyo. We sat in the hut and discussed our prospects and possibilities in low voices. There was little point, we agreed, in trying to get away during daylight. Not only was there the sound of fairly constant activity in the village generally, but we had a savage standing on guard outside the hut. He had keen hearing, too. When Kelly pulled at a section of the wall to see if there was a chance of making a hole in it, he was inside right away, threatening us with his club.

The only hope lay in waiting until dark. There was really no reason to think our chances would be a great deal better then, particularly since we were going to have to escape into the forest at night, but they must be a bit better.

It was a long and miserable day. We were brought neither food nor water. The few tomatoes we had succeeded in eating had not gone far toward satisfying hunger, and we were soon thirsty again as well. But we were also exhausted and dozed off from time to time.

I was awakened from one such doze by someone coming into the hut. A savage said something unintelligible and gestured that we should go outside. I followed Kelly and Sunyo, dazed and apprehensive. More savages were there, some with ropes which they used to tie our hands behind our backs, not very gently. It was early evening, the sky red in the west but dark blue overhead. So much, I thought, for our project of a night escape.

Once our hands were tied, we were marched out of the village along a track that led the opposite way to the vegetable patch. It was very narrow and overgrown in places. A couple of savages went in front of us and half a dozen behind. Even with free hands it would have been hopeless to try to get away. I thought of my fantasy of getting to Southampton, my daydream about Mr. Sherrin and my father and Miranda. Right now I was ready to settle for getting the ropes off my hands and something to eat.

It was a long journey, with the light draining out of the sky and the forest seeming to press continuously closer. I stumbled once and fell and got a smack across the shoulders from a cudgel to rouse me. I wondered what awaited us at the end of the trek but was too numb and exhausted to bother much. The nagging ache in my belly was almost lost in a need to lie down and forget everything. I faltered, and the cudgel hit me again.

Then as we rounded a bend, there was a light ahead much brighter than the pale moonlight under which we had been traveling for the last hour. I saw a fire, a huge blaze crackling against the dark screen of trees. I could hear voices as well. Our savages called out and were greeted in return. They pushed us forward and we stood, blinking, in the glare.

It was difficult to tell how many there were in this new band, but more than a score, I thought. They were all wearing trousers and shirts made from green cloth. Their faces, when they looked at us, seemed to show more contempt than curiosity. One of them said something and the others laughed, not pleasantly.

Then a different voice called, "Bring them over here. Let me have a look at them."

But the voice was surprising; it had a city accent. We were taken round the campfire to where a man sat, cross-legged, on the ground. He rose to his feet, and I saw that he was very tall, well over six feet, with a curly black beard touched in places with white, and a big hooked nose. As he stared at us, unsmiling, I felt the last remnants of my strength draining out of my legs.

"City boys," he said. The contempt was very plain. "Which city?"

He was looking at me and I told him, "London. But the others . . ."

"What about them?"

I pointed to them. "Sunyo's from Kyoto, Kelly from Jacksonville."

He seemed more interested. "Explain that."

I told him briefly about the island and our escape. His face showed nothing. In the end he said,

"So you ran away because life was hard. That may not have been very wise of you."

We did not answer.

He stared at us, his face hawklike. He said, "In fact, it's something you may well regret. The Outlands are no place for city boys. Do you know me, Clive of London?"

I shook my head as the bearded face gazed cheerlessly into mine.

"The other two won't have heard my name, but you may have. They call me Wild Jack."

7

WE WERE TAKEN TO ANOTHER HUT AND
left there. In this village, as in the first,
huts were built round the sides of a clearing, under the shelter of the trees, but these were
much more substantial. The logs which formed the
walls were thicker and more solidly bound, and the
hut had a proper door. We heard the sound of an
iron bolt being slammed home on the far side.

It was pitch dark inside. I felt my way to a wall
and leaned against it. Kelly said, "OK, so who is
Wild Jack?"

I scarcely knew what to think myself. I said, "It's

a story the servants tell—the nurse-women, anyway. He's a kind of bogeyman. They talk about Wild Jack coming up from the Outlands and stealing children. It's just a way of making kids behave themselves—at least, I thought so."

Sunyo said, "We have a story something like it in Japan. But he's called Hairy Ainu. Some of the tales are very bloodthirsty."

"Some of the ones about Wild Jack are. There's a song he's supposed to sing:

> *"Fee fo fi fan,*
> *I smell the blood of a city man."*

"Our servants talk about Bloody Bill," Kelly said. "I guess it's the same legend everywhere."

"But this Wild Jack is real," Sunyo said. "He seems to be the chief of this lot."

"He called himself Wild Jack," Kelly said. "Talking big. He's just a savage."

I said slowly, "Not just a savage. He speaks good city English."

"Are you telling us you believe that guff?" Kelly

asked. "Stealing babies and all that? You ever hear of a baby being stolen?"

I said with heat, "No, of course, I don't believe it. But he's not an ordinary savage. He could be more dangerous. Why does he call himself Wild Jack, anyway? He's obviously some kind of renegade."

Kelly started to reply, but Sunyo cut across.

"Whoever he is, he doesn't look friendly. We should be thinking of escape instead of wasting our time in argument."

"Sure," Kelly said, "but how? We can't even see the walls."

"We can feel round them," Sunyo said. "There was a weak spot in the other hut. We might be able to find one in this."

At least it gave us something to do. I groped my way along the wall, which seemed discouragingly substantial. At one point I stumbled across Kelly, and we exchanged a few sharp words. Sunyo was telling us to shut up when we heard the bolt being drawn.

The door was pushed open, showing the light of the campfire and another light much nearer where a man held up a burning torch. A figure came past him and I saw, with surprise, that it was a girl.

She was roughly our age and Sunyo's height but, of course, much slimmer. She was dressed in green like the men, wearing a shirt open at the neck and long pants. Her hair was black and thick, shoulder length, and I could see that her face was very brown—I had never seen a girl with so brown a face. It had a hard, unfriendly look, though her features were regular enough.

"Wild Jack sends you your supper," she said.

Her voice was hard also, though she, too, spoke in city English. She had very white teeth.

"If you were expecting a feast," she said, "you're going to be disappointed. We don't waste food in the Outlands. Wild Jack will decide what to do with you tomorrow."

She handed over a pot and a loaf of bread. I took the bread and Kelly the pot. The girl said scornfully, with a shrug of her shoulders, "Sleep as well as you can, city boys."

She went out. The door was slammed and the bolt driven home, leaving us once more in the dark.

Kelly said, "It's water in the pot. She was right about it not being a feast."

I divided the loaf by breaking it into pieces, doing my best to make equal shares. I gave Kelly and Sunyo their rations, and Kelly passed the pot round. He said, "Go easy on it. We don't know when we'll be getting any more."

"I'm not a fool," I said, sipping.

In fact I was not too sure of that. I had a distinct feeling I had given Kelly the largest share of bread and kept the smallest for myself. Then he made things worse by saying to Sunyo, "You take some of mine. It's days since you had anything to eat."

Ashamed, I was about to offer some to Sunyo, too, but he said, "No. I'm all right. Listen, I had a good look at the walls in the light of the torch. I noticed a spot where it might be weaker. Eat the bread, and we'll see what we can do about it."

I wolfed mine. Kelly finished his soon after, but Sunyo went on eating slowly. The sound of his chewing was maddening; I was still ravenously hungry. At last he finished, and we joined him in investigating the weakness he thought he had found. It was high up, where the wall and roof joined at a corner, and we could reach it only by taking turns for one of us to give another a back. Sunyo had first go, with Kelly supporting him, and then I helped Kelly up. When it was my turn, I felt for and found the hole and pulled at it with my fingers.

The wood was rotten, and you could enlarge it to some extent, but beyond a certain point you were blocked by the ropes which secured the logs.

I said, gasping, "If we had a knife . . ."

Sunyo was underneath me. Kelly said, "How about a thermo-lance? And a helicopter standing by on the roof? No sense in going in for small fantasies."

I ignored him and spoke to Sunyo. "I don't think I'm getting anywhere."

"Let me have another try."

I surrendered my place to him willingly, and he worked away patiently for what seemed hours.

Kelly said, "Want me to spell you?"

"No." Sunyo's voice was tired and final. "We're wasting our time. It's too solid to get through."

Kelly said, "I agree. Let's try to get some rest. Whatever's coming to us tomorrow, there's no sense in meeting it deadbeat. I'll take the air-sprung four-poster bed next to the big window. You guys find your own."

This hut, too, had a floor of beaten earth, but I was asleep almost as soon as I settled down on it. And almost as soon as I was asleep, I was awake again and doubled up with stomach pains; the bread had been new, and I had eaten it much too fast. I lay and writhed for what seemed hours before eventually drifting into exhausted sleep. I had the impression it was a couple of minutes later that I was wakened again, by the door being pushed open. I looked up muzzily and saw daylight. I saw, too, a figure framed in the doorway and recognized the curly black beard and hooked nose of the man who called himself Wild Jack.

I struggled painfully to my feet; Kelly and Sunyo were already standing. Wild Jack came into the hut. He looked from us to the hole we had scratched in the corner of the roof and laughed.

"So the mice have been trying to escape from their trap! It looks as though their teeth weren't quite sharp enough. But you wouldn't expect much of city mice, would you?"

Although he spoke good English, his voice had a rough edge I didn't like, and his laugh did not have much mirth in it. He said, "Get outside."

We went blinking into the clearing. The sun had risen above the trees on the far side, and the sky was sharply blue against the green. We were watched by figures who looked no more friendly than their leader. From the direction of the campfire came the sizzle of frying bacon and a smell that almost made me faint with hunger.

"We didn't invite you," Wild Jack said, "and you might have been wiser not to come. Since you are here, you've no choice but to make the best of it, though I'm not sure your best is going to be quite good enough. Still, it will pass an amusing few minutes, and as we already have another candidate for the ordeal, it won't really waste our time."

He turned to a man who stood near him whom I had already noticed with some apprehension. He almost contrived to make Wild Jack look small, being inches taller and massive too, broad in both girth and shoulders.

"Is our little traitor ready for judgment, Daniel?" Wild Jack asked.

The big man nodded silently and snapped his fingers. Two men brought up a third. This one was as small as Daniel was huge, a wiry fellow not much more than five feet in height, with gingery hair and beard and a sharp, terrified face. His hands were roped behind him. His eyes fastened on Wild Jack in desperate appeal.

"They told lies on me, Jack." His voice was thin with terror. "You know I'd never let you down. I wouldn't betray you. You know that."

"Well in that case," Wild Jack said, "you have no cause to worry, do you?"

His tone, though, was the opposite of reassuring, and the little man looked worse than ever. Some of those standing around laughed, and I heard another laugh on a higher note. I looked and saw the girl who had brought us our miserable supper. She noticed my glance and smiled in a way that made me want to murder her. Both she and the men wore expressions of looking forward to an amusing show. Amusing for them, perhaps, but certainly not for the gingery man or for us.

When our hands were being bound again, I realized that we were not going to be given any food. It may seem strange, but, quite apart from my hunger, this was the most frightening thing of all. I remembered the girl's words when she had given us the loaf of bread. "We don't waste food in the Outlands." Recalling them made me shiver; not wasting food on people who had not long to live provided a very reasonable explanation.

Horses were brought into the clearing. These, like the pigs, were familiar to me only from pictures; unlike Kelly with his race course, we had no horses in London. Wild Jack and his followers mounted, while we three and the gingery man were tied to a rope whose end was fastened to the saddle of one of the horses. Then, on an order from Wild Jack, they moved off along a trail leading out of the camp, and we had to stumble after them.

The trail was very rough in places, and although the horses were only walking, they set a pace uncomfortably fast for us on foot. I was second in line, directly behind the gingery man, who mumbled unhappily to himself much of the time.

The sun, I noticed, was on our right, which meant that we were heading north. Not that it made any difference, since all this was Wild Jack's kingdom and one place no better than another. I heard a distant hum of an engine and looked up at the narrow stretch of sky that was visible between the surrounding trees. I did not see the airship—not that that made any difference either. No one could help us.

The trail came out at last into the open, with the next stretch of forest sixty or seventy feet farther on. In between, the ground fell into a ravine.

Wild Jack and his companions dismounted and tethered their horses to outlying trees. I felt a fresh qualm as the four of us were prodded forward and was relieved as we got nearer to the rocky edge to see that the ravine was no more than about ten feet deep. Bushes grew thickly along the bottom. Not far away, too, there was a rope bridge connecting this side with the other.

It consisted of a kind of ladder at the bottom, with short pieces of wood tied into a double rope at intervals of a couple of inches. Several feet above it a single rope, fastened to trees on either side, was presumably meant to serve as a hand support.

One of the men untied our hands, and Wild Jack said, "This is where we have our little test. It's quite a simple one. Merely a matter of crossing the bridge to get to the other side. Do you think you can manage that, city boys?"

The bridge swayed slightly in a breeze. If this was what Wild Jack called an ordeal, he must have a poor opinion of city boys indeed. But the gingery man was still shivering with fear.

"You don't look much dismayed," Wild Jack said. "That's a good thing. But we mustn't make it too easy for you, must we? Thomas!"

A man stepped forward with a knife. It dazzled in sunlight as he slashed at the upper rope, which fell into the ravine, briefly threshing the bushes.

"How do you fancy your chances now?" Wild Jack asked.

I fancied them a good deal less. There remained only the narrow rope ladder; it would require quite a feat of balancing to cross without support above. But I reflected that if one did fall, it would be a distance of no more than eight or nine feet. I thought of something else, too. Wild Jack and his men were all here on top. If one were to drop and run for it . . . it was a chance that might be worth taking. I glanced at Kelly and Sunyo and wondered if the same thought had crossed their minds. The little gingery man was drawing quick, gusty breaths of what seemed like panic.

"Just one other small thing," Wild Jack said. He smiled. "This ravine has a name. It's called Taipan Canyon."

I had no idea what he was talking about and wasn't interested. It had occurred to me that it would not be possible for all three of us to make a break for it by dropping into the ravine, because the moment one did so, it would alert Wild Jack and his men. Unless we contrived to jump together, before we were ordered to cross? I wondered how I could get the idea over to the others.

"The taipan," Wild Jack said, "was not originally a native of this country. It came from Australia. But there were specimens in zoos here, and during the Breakdown some got loose. Perhaps only one female, but if so she laid eggs. And, like certain other animals, the taipan has flourished in the Outlands. In this ravine, in particular."

We looked down. There was nothing to be seen but the bushes, their tops rippled by the breeze. Wild Jack smiled again.

"You won't see any. They're not very big, and they stay close to the ground. But they're fast movers. Taipans, city boys, are snakes—in fact, the deadliest snakes in the world. There's no antidote to their venom, and they kill within a couple of minutes. What's more, they have a very strong objection to being disturbed."

We looked at him. He spoke convincingly, but it could be a tale to frighten us. I looked down again and saw nothing. Wild Jack said, "Our traitor has priority."

The gingery man was pushed forward toward the bridge, almost gibbering with fear. He gulped before he could speak.

"I swear I'm no traitor, Jack! I swear it. It was all lies, lies. . . ."

The man with the knife held its point close to his chest. Wild Jack said, "If that's true, you'll come through the ordeal, won't you? An honest man won't fall."

I asked myself, sickened, if such a barbarity could be believed? But these were the Outlands, not the civilized world we knew. The men were grinning, and I saw the girl grin with them. They were savages, capable of anything.

The gingery man dropped to his knees. He cried, "Please, Jack. For old times' sake. . . ."

In a cold, indifferent voice, Wild Jack said, "We don't have all day to waste. There are other candidates as well as you. Get him on the bridge, Thomas."

The knife was turned to his back, and when it pricked him, the gingery man took a hasty step forward and put one foot on the bridge. It swayed, and he drew back. There was an ugly shout of laughter from the men in green, and the knife pricked him again between the shoulder blades. This time he started to walk across.

The bridge twisted as he went on, and he hesitated and began to wobble. His expression was agonized; I could see his mouth working furiously. The more he struggled to retain his balance, the more the bridge swayed. With a wild shriek he fell, somersaulting through the air to land among the bushes.

There was a cheer from the men in green, repeated as he scrambled to his feet and started to run for the far side. He had covered three or four yards when, with another sharper cry, he dropped. We could see him writhing and clutching his leg just above the ankle.

His voice came to us, thin and despairing: "Help me. . . ."

He managed to get up a second time and hobble on, but he was clearly in great pain. He staggered and fell again, and this time did not rise. Wild Jack's men laughed as he struggled, and roared with approval when he finally lay still.

Silence followed. Wild Jack said, "So he was a traitor. I knew it. Now for the city boys. Who goes first?"

While I was trying to make up my mind to step forward, Kelly did so.

"I'll go."

Wild Jack stared at him. "Right. Take it gently. And if you do fall, run very fast. No one's outrun the snakes yet, but there's no harm in trying."

Kelly did not answer but went straight to the bridge. It swayed as he stepped on it, and he hesitated briefly, then walked slowly on.

Halfway across, the bridge swayed more sharply, moved perhaps by a stiffening in the breeze. Kelly bent down and rested his hands on the ladder. He regained his balance, stood up, and went on carefully to the far side.

"One over," Wild Jack said. He did not try to hide his disappointment. "Who's next?"

I was ready this time, but Sunyo was ahead of me. He looked straight at Wild Jack, with an expression of contempt and anger. Wild Jack nodded. Sunyo turned from him and headed for the bridge.

There was no hesitation. He went with assurance, step by steady step, and did not halt until he reached the end. Kelly put his hand out, and Sunyo joined him on firm ground.

"Fair enough," Wild Jack said. The disappointment was very plain now, and his men were silent. "That still leaves one."

The bridge looked narrower and flimsier than ever. I glanced down at the thicket, where the body of the gingery man lay between two bushes. It lay quite still. The breeze gusted, and the bridge moved with it.

"Well?" Wild Jack asked. "Do you need a pricking on, city boy?"

I moved before the man with the knife could come at me. I caught sight of the girl's face, fiercely intent, as I reached the bridge, and thought for a fleeting moment of Miranda's very different one.

And I thought of something else as I stood poised to step on the ladder. Kelly and Sunyo had reached the other side, and the ravine now lay between them and Wild Jack's men. This was their best chance to escape; they could be deep inside the forest before anyone could get there.

I called out, "Run for it! Get away while you can."

Neither moved. Kelly called back, "We'll wait for you, Clive."

Idiots, I thought; but I had other things to think about. I stepped onto the bridge and felt it move under me. Instinctively my eyes went down. The ladder was about a foot in width—not a lot when it hung swaying over a nasty drop with poisonous snakes at the bottom.

When I stopped, there was a roar of derision from behind me. I started forward again, placing my feet carefully, one in front of the other. Looking down made me dizzy, and the bridge's swaying seemed worse when it oscillated against the green of the canyon floor. I took a deep breath, raised my head, and looked ahead, concentrating on the watching figures of Kelly and Sunyo on the far side. I felt for my footholds, step by step. I knew I must be making progress, but the distance before me seemed to get no less.

When I was three-quarters of the way across, the breeze blew up again, making the bridge move sharply under my feet. Somehow I managed to get down, as Kelly had done, and hold on with my hands. I felt sweat pouring from me. It was a long time before I dared stand and go on.

Very slowly I approached the end of the bridge. Perhaps ten more steps—nine, eight. . . . The breeze gusted even more severely, and as I fought to keep my balance, I knew that this time I was not going to make it.

So I stopped trying to balance and, throwing caution to the wind, ran along the twisting narrow span. I managed several steps as it jerked and buckled under me, but the end was still some feet off when I knew I was losing my footing. Desperately I jumped and saw Kelly and Sunyo with their hands out, reaching for me. For a moment my feet scrabbled on the edge of the drop, but Kelly's hand had my arm firmly. Between them, they pulled me up.

I gasped, "Run for it now! While we have a chance."

"No good," Sunyo said.

He pointed at the trees on this side. Figures in

green were moving toward us. Wild Jack had taken precautions after all; his men were on both sides of the ravine.

I was still shivering from the crossing. I looked back at the bridge and saw Wild Jack coming over. He made it look easy.

He was laughing, and my fears returned. We had survived the ordeal which had killed the gingery man, but did that mean anything? Would someone who had thought up something as sadistic as that let us go after passing his test? I could not believe it.

He jumped from the bridge to stand beside us.

"Well done, city boys." He turned and looked down into the ravine. "And well done, Ben! All right, you can get up now."

I followed his glance to where the gingery man lay still between the bushes. As I did so, the "dead man" stood up and walked toward us, grinning.

8

KELLY SAID, "THEN THERE ARE NO SNAKES IN the ravine?"

"I wouldn't swear to that," Wild Jack said. "There will very likely be grass snakes. And perhaps an adder or two."

"Are they poisonous?" I asked.

The support rope had been replaced, and we had crossed back to our starting point. The girl was standing near. She said with a laugh, "You don't learn much in those cities of yours!"

Wild Jack said, "You mustn't be too hard on them, Joan. They don't have much chance." He spoke to me: "Grass snakes are quite harmless. Adders have poison fangs, but they won't attack a man unless he's fool enough to step on them. And it's rare for anyone to die from the bite of an adder."

"That stuff about taipans," Kelly said, "—you made all that up?"

"No. The taipan really is an Australian snake, and it's just as deadly as I said it was. And there were probably some in the snake houses of some zoos before the Breakdown. There may even have been one or two that escaped, though I don't think it's likely. It's a lot more unlikely that any would have survived. England is a vastly different place from Australia."

Ben, the gingery man, was grinning.

I said, "So he just faked being bitten? He did it very well."

"He ought to be able to," Wild Jack said. "He used to be an actor in the days when he was a city man." He put his hand on Ben's shoulder. "And I think he misses the actor's life a bit now and then, if the truth were known."

There had been a feeling of recognition at the back of my mind before this, but I had dismissed it as ridiculous. I said, "Of course, I remember! That

TV series about World War II—you played the comic private."

"A fan again, after all these years," he said, full of mock delight. "How it brings it all back! Saddle me a horse, Jack, and I'll be off to Philadelphia in the morning."

Kelly and I laughed. The sense of relief made me inclined to laugh at anything. Sunyo's expression, though, was one of bitter anger. He looked at Wild Jack.

"So the ordeal was just a joke, a clever bit of playacting. Why? For your amusement?"

Wild Jack shook his head.

"No. We do have a sense of humor in the Outlands which may be a bit different from what you are used to in the cities, but it doesn't include terrifying people without a good reason."

"So what is the reason?" Sunyo asked.

"You're not the first to have come into the Outlands from the cities. There are some who take one look at the forest and run back home to the shelter of their walls. Others persevere and make contact with us or with people like us. They usually say they want to live with us, but they often don't understand what it involves. It could take a long time for them to realize they aren't suited to our life, and all that time they're a drag on us—or worse. When they do finally decide to go back to their cozy cities, they could take information with them."

"Would that matter?" Kelly asked.

"It might. Anyway, we've had to find a means of weeding out unsuitable ones at the beginning. Quite simply, you can't live in the Outlands without reasonable physical ability and also strength of mind. The bridge tests the first, and the tale about the taipans the second."

"And if we had failed . . . ," I said.

"Southampton city is not far away. We would have taken you there and left you."

"And if we should want to go back, now that we've passed your test?"

Wild Jack shrugged. "No one will stop you. We only want men who are volunteers. We are all free in the Outlands."

Kelly nodded enthusiastically, Sunyo more dubiously. Wild Jack said, "First things first. You've earned something better than bread and water, and I should think you could do justice to it."

. . .

We were taken back to camp in better style than we had gone out, riding on the saddles of the horsemen. I jogged behind the vast bulk of Daniel, who appeared quite amiable now, though I still found him a bit frightening. In the clearing other men in green had breakfast waiting for us.

Really it was more like a feast. The bacon tasted as good as it had smelled, and there were piles of spicy sausages, as many eggs as you could eat, loaves of bread that was coarse and brown but smelled good and tasted better, jars of golden butter . . . with pots of buttermilk to wash it all down. We gorged ourselves until we lay, dazed with food, under the trees.

Later we wandered round the camp, exploring. It was much bigger than I had thought, consisting of a number of different clearings connected by short trails through the trees. In one clearing, the tree trunks had wooden boxes about eighteen inches square nailed to them. Fat pigeons sat on and around some of the boxes, and others showed a glimpse of beak through round holes in the sides. Wild Jack came along while we were looking.

"So you've found my messengers," he said. "How do you like them?"

Kelly echoed, "Messengers?"

"Since we have no radio or TV, we must communicate by more primitive methods. That one goes back a long, long way—to the Romans or maybe earlier. They're carrier pigeons. As far as they are concerned, this is home. If you take them away, even hundreds of miles, they will fly back to their boxes. And if you write a message very small—by scratching signs on a leaf, say—and tie it to one of their legs, they will bring it with them."

"That gets messages here," Kelly said. "How about the other way?"

"Simple. We keep birds from different parts of the country in cages. They take messages to wherever they were born and bred."

"So there are more camps like yours," Sunyo said. "And other Wild Jacks?"

"Other camps, yes." He grinned. "But only one Wild Jack."

"Your people are different from the savages," Sunyo said. "Aren't they?"

"Savages? That's a city word. And not one that I'm fond of."

"We mean the guys who caught us and brought us to you," Kelly said. "Whatever you call them."

"I would call them human beings," Wild Jack said. "As we are."

"So are the people of the cities," I said.

Wild Jack looked at me. "True. Let's say then that the people of the Outlands are free human beings."

"We're free in the cities, too."

"So free that you got sent to a punishment island for nothing?"

"That was a mistake. Mistakes can happen anywhere."

"True again. And your friends?" He turned toward Kelly and Sunyo. "Why were they sent to the island?"

They told their stories and he listened. At the end he said, "Kelly got into trouble for trying to stop a schoolroom tyrant bullying another boy. And Sunyo's father had the pictures of his ancestors— pictures which he loved, and which did no one any harm—destroyed by the police of his city. Freedom?"

I said, "There may be a few things wrong."

"A few things? Let's have a look at your own case again. Perhaps it was a mistake sending you to the island, but what about the charge itself? You were supposed to have talked about the rights of servants. You didn't, but what if you had? Do you regard that as something bad enough to justify them sending you—or anyone else—to a place like that?"

"It's done to prevent civil disturbance. There have been servants who have given trouble in the past. The police don't want to have it happen again."

"Then you admit that the servants aren't free in your cities?"

"No, but . . ."

"But what?"

"They don't want freedom. They're quite happy as they are."

"Are they? Have you asked them?"

"I don't need to," I said stubbornly. I thought of Bobby. "You can see they're contented."

"And if you did ask, you could scarcely expect to get an honest answer, could you? Because you are one of the masters, born to rule the lower orders. Is that fair, do you think?"

I was sure there must be an answer to that but could not think of one. I only said, "Fairness has nothing to do with it."

"You're right, but perhaps it should have. It isn't just the servants, is it? What about the poor despised savages in the Outlands? Every one of those cities of yours has an energy tower providing its inhabitants with all the heat and power they want. Power to work the machines which make city life so easy. In the Outlands there's a constant battle against nature for everything. We have no power, no machines. We're forced to live by the strength of our arms and the sweat of our brows."

Sunyo said, "But do you envy the city people their easy life? If so, why did you, a city man, choose to live in the Outlands instead?"

"I didn't say I chose." Wild Jack laughed. "But you are right, my friend from the East! I like this life better than my old one, for all its hardships and dangers. Perhaps simply because of that freedom we were talking about. Even if the people of the cities believe they themselves are free, they are served by slaves. Their luxury and ease rest on a selfishness worse than anything the world has known."

"It's not selfishness," I argued, "to want to pro-
tect yourself."

"Yourself or your riches? But it isn't a question
that will be solved by argument. We're better stick-
ing to practical things—like my birds, which need
feeding."

He put his hand in the pocket in the front of his
trousers and brought it out full of corn.

He called, "Come then, my pretties. Come and eat."

A couple of pigeons, blue-gray in color, flew over
and perched, one on his wrist and the other on his
fingers. He watched them, smiling, while they pecked
at the seeds.

The birds' wings, already gleaming in the sunlight, dazzled in brighter colors as they rose, flap-
ping, at the arrival of a newcomer. This one was
reddish-brown, and it pushed the others away and
settled confidently on Wild Jack's thumb. He ruffled
its neck feathers with his free hand, and it pecked his
fingers for a moment, though neither angrily nor in
alarm, before going on feeding.

"Rusty's my favorite," Wild Jack said.

He put his hand up near his face, and the bird
pecked at his curly beard. It was hard to believe this

was the face which a few hours before had looked so frightening.

"You know it, too, don't you?" Wild Jack said. He watched the bird, smiling. "He's our only one of this color. But apart from that, he's been a good carrier. He has carried many a message for me in his day."

"Why do you call him Rusty?" Sunyo asked.

"Because he's red, not because he's slow! He's getting on now, but in his younger days there weren't many winged creatures that could outfly him."

I said, "Would he come to me?"

"Try him."

He tipped corn into my hand, disturbing the bird. It rose fluttering in the air and then came back to feed from my palm. The pecking beak tickled my skin.

Sunyo said, "Even though you say they are free human beings too, there *is* a difference between your men and others in the Outlands, isn't there? The ones the city people call savages."

"You're very persistent," Wild Jack said, "but it's not a bad quality. Those they call savages are people whose ancestors have lived for generations in the Outlands. Some of our men come from them, and they get on well with us for the most part." He smiled. "When they find strangers raiding their vegetable patches, they bring them to us to deal with. But most of us are like Ben and Daniel and myself—men from the cities who have chosen the forest for reasons which seemed good to them."

"What was your reason?" Kelly asked.

He paused before saying, "It's over and done with. But it was a good reason, I thought. And I have found better reasons since. No, we are not savages, whatever the city people say. Outlaws is a better name, because we live outside their laws. Though we have laws of our own we abide by—and better laws than theirs, I think."

Rusty was pecking at the last few grains. I risked tickling his neck, and he let me, pecking at my thumb gently.

Wild Jack said, "He seems to have taken to you, Clive. I must watch out, or I may lose a bird."

Later we were shown the weapons used by the men in green. They had knives and heavy sticks and also bows and arrows. The bows were made from the wood of yew trees; it split easily, Wild Jack told us, but at the same time was the strongest wood in the forest. The bows were strung with thin strips of hide. Wild Jack's bow was as tall as he was, and he was an inch or two over six feet. The wood had been polished to a high gloss, and the string twanged musically when he flicked it.

He took an arrow from the quiver at his belt and handed that and the bow to me.

"Shall we see if you have the makings of a bowman?"

"Where shall I aim?"

"Anywhere you like, as long as it's not at anything that can take hurt."

I fitted the arrow into the string and tried to bend the bow. It was a lot stiffer than I had expected. By straining hard I managed to pull the string back a few inches, and released the arrow. It traveled weakly through the air to land in the dust a few yards away.

"You will need practice," Wild Jack said. "How about you, Kelly?"

Kelly's effort was an improvement on mine, but not by much. Sunyo followed. When he took the bow, he first felt the smooth wood with his hands, gently rubbing it, caressing it almost. Before fitting the arrow he took a slow, deep breath; his face had the fixed, distant look it had when he was meditating. Then very slowly he bent the bow and shot the arrow. It carried at least twice the distance of Kelly's.

Wild Jack said approvingly, "We shan't have much trouble turning you into a bowman. But you have to have trueness as well as strength." He pointed across the clearing. "Try aiming at that tree."

It was an old oak, huge in girth. Sunyo took another arrow and shot it. He missed the tree by a yard at least.

Wild Jack took the bow himself.

"The sapling that stands apart, next to the ragged bush."

It was much farther than the oak, about seventy feet from where we stood. Muscles rippled along his arm as he drew back the string.

"The height of a man's head."

The arrow hissed through the air, and we followed him across the clearing. The sapling offered a target perhaps two inches wide, and the arrow's head was embedded in it dead center. The shaft stuck out on a level with Wild Jack's brow.

• • •

During the days that followed we joined in the life of the men in green. This included learning to ride on horseback, something we did very badly to start with. We fell off in turn, and at the end of the day our legs ached and the insides of our thighs were rubbed sore. Ben gave us a foul-smelling ointment which lessened the smart, and during the next day or two we began to get the knack of horsemanship.

But it was not all riding. There was a river a few minutes from the camp, fed by the stream from which the outlaws took their water. It was well supplied with fish, and Ben and Daniel showed us their ways of catching them, using rods and lines with ingenious baits and hooks on the end. The rods were long and supple, and they cast the lines far out over the tumbling· green waters. The pile of fish grew steadily in the wicker baskets beside us. The sky that day alternated between sun and threatening clouds, and while we were fishing, a sudden shower drenched us to the skin. But then the sun came out again, drying and warming us.

Kelly, who had handed his rod over to Sunyo, said, "Boy, this is the life."

Daniel smiled. He was a slow-moving, genial man who boasted of laziness. He was very strong. There was a story that when a companion broke a leg he had carried him ten miles back to camp, without even looking tired at the end. He said to Kelly, "It's not always like this. The sun doesn't always shine, and it isn't always summer. There's also autumn and winter—hard times and cold times. And work as well as play. Even I can't always avoid it."

Kelly said, "Sure, I understand that. But it's all so different from what we were told about the Outlands. They told us about the savages, and the terrible lives they had to lead—grubbing for food, being eaten by wild animals when they weren't starving to death." He looked at the heap of fish in the basket. "They're going to taste pretty good. The food back home was nowhere like as good as we've been getting here."

Daniel smiled again. "Appetite is the best sauce, and appetite is something the Outlands do guarantee you. But fish from the river are better than the kind they breed in the energy tower coolant pools, too—I'll grant you that. Do you think we have enough for supper yet?"

I had one tugging at the end of my line. The sensation of its quick, dragging weight was strange and incredibly exciting. I said, "Not yet!"

Ben was stretched out in the sun, with his eyes closed. He said sleepily, "Don't hurry him. We have plenty of mouths to feed, and I would say the three latest can do more than their share. They're almost in your class, Daniel."

The following day most of the men went off on a deer hunt. We were expecting to go with them, but Wild Jack said no; a deer hunt was a serious business, and anyone as inexperienced as we were would only be a nuisance. There would, he pointed out, be other hunts in the future.

The camp seemed weirdly empty with only a few men left behind—mostly those with minor ailments or disabilities, like the one whose leg had mended badly after a break so that he walked with a heavy limp; he was the one Daniel had carried back to camp. The day was hot, and in the early afternoon we pondered what to do. It was Kelly's suggestion that we go down to the river again, not to fish but to swim.

The girl Joan had been left behind also. We had not had much to do with her so far, but I found myself disliking her more and more. There had been several occasions when she made sarcastic comments on our skills or lack of them, and I had come to loathe the sound of her laughter. It tended to echo in my mind even when she wasn't there.

But overhearing us make our plans, she announced her intention of joining us. I thought nothing to this and said as much. She looked at me with an air of detached contempt and addressed Kelly. "I'm coming with you. All right?"

He shrugged and nodded. On the way to the river, while she was leading the way with Sunyo, I whispered my protests, and he said, "All right, I know how you feel. But you must admit she seems kind of important to the outlaws. They all make a fuss over her. She's sort of a mascot, I guess. Even though she's a pain in the neck, I reckon we have no real choice about something like this."

She insisted on showing us a place she said was good for swimming, a quarter of a mile upstream from the fishing spot. I was relieved that at least she did not suggest coming in with us but was apparently content to sit on the bank and watch, though I found that irritating enough.

The rest of us dived in and messed about for a time. It was very different from the heated swimming pools of the cities: more fun, Kelly claimed, though I was not so sure. I missed the diving boards and slides, and it was disconcerting to put your foot down and touch mud or a sharp stone.

In the past, swimming had been one of my favorite sports, and I had been reckoned to be good at it. Since we had been with the outlaws, Kelly had proved a better horseman than I, and Sunyo a better archer. For that matter, I had come worst out of the test of crossing the ravine. It would be a nice change to have something at which I could excel.

So I challenged Kelly and Sunyo to a race. The river ran straight for some distance, and a willow overhung the water at the point where it curved away to the right.

I said, "Race you to the willow. OK?"

I had a lead right from the start and increased it steadily. When I put my hand on a root of the tree growing out of the bank, Kelly was five yards behind me, with Sunyo trailing.

Joan had followed us along the bank. She looked down at me and said, "Not bad, for a city boy." I ignored the remark and climbed out. "I'll race you back."

"No, thanks."

"I'll give you time to get your breath."

I was stung by that. "I don't need to get my breath!"

"All right, then."

She kicked off her sandals, pulled off shirt and pants, and stood in briefs and breast band. She looked at Kelly, who had also come up on the bank.

"Give us a start."

I was rather proud of the racing start I made, but when I looked, she was ahead of me. I was using the crawl stroke, and I put everything into it. For a while I thought I was closing the gap; then, her brown arms cleaving the water as though effortlessly, she drew farther ahead. She beat me by at least the distance I had beaten Kelly, if not more.

I was fed up with myself, furiously angry with her. The other two complimented her on her swimming, but I could not bring myself to say anything. The sun

was hot, and we all sat on the bank, drying ourselves. I remained silent, but Kelly and Sunyo talked, mostly about the men in green. Kelly went on and on about Wild Jack—what a great guy he was. I was feeling choked with everything connected with the Outlands, Wild Jack included. I said, "Great—for a savage."

Joan turned on me quickly. "Shut up, city boy. Or I'll shut you up."

I laughed. "Go ahead!"

"Don't tempt me." Her voice was cold, but her eyes flashed fury. "I was reared in the Outlands, not in one of your soft cities. I can fight as well as swim. If you want that delicate city nose of yours rubbed in the mud, just go on talking about savages."

I remembered the way those arms of hers had cut through water; although slim in build, she was obviously very strong. I wasn't afraid, but I had a suspicion that if I did get into a fight with her it could prove both tough and inconclusive. And she had made me look enough of a fool as it was.

So I shrugged. "One thing we don't do in the cities is fight girls."

She laughed. "Right! You don't have to here

either, as long as you don't insult Wild Jack."

I ignored that. It was Sunyo who said, with an open interest unusual for him, "You defend Wild Jack very fiercely."

"Not that he needs it." She shook her head, laughing again. "But if I do, why not? He's my father."

That night they roasted a deer over the campfire, and we had spells of turning the handle of the spit which was mounted on a block of wood alongside. The work was hot and tiring, but we had the smell of roasting meat to spur us, and pots of ale were brought to quench our thirst. Afterward came the feasting, and later still the men in green sang, singly or in unison. I did not know the songs, but some of them had a strange, almost haunting familiarity.

It was pleasant, anyway, to listen, full of roast venison, with the fire blazing against the dark screen of trees and the sky overhead deepening from blue to purple. Ben told a comic story in verse, with snatches of song, about an outlaw who got lost in the forest. The others had obviously heard it many times before but still found it very funny. A lot of it was lost on us, but we laughed with the rest.

As the fire crumbled into embers, Wild Jack came to talk to us.

"Are you boys all right?"

Full and drowsy, we said we were.

He said, "I reckon you've had long enough with us."

Kelly said quickly, "You're not sending us back? I thought we could stay here."

"Long enough to decide if you want to stay, I meant. There's a city only a few hours' ride away. We could take you there tomorrow."

"I'm staying," Kelly said. He added, "If you're willing to have me, that is. Do I take an oath or something, sir?"

Wild Jack grinned. "No oaths and no 'sirs.' I've told you, we're all free men in the Outlands. What about you, from the land of the rising sun?"

Sunyo said, "I want to stay."

Wild Jack turned to me. "Well, Clive?"

A good deal went through my mind. The Outlands had proved very different from what I had expected— different and, despite what I had said on the river bank, a lot better. But, thinking of Joan, I thought of Miranda and then of the things I had left behind in the city. I remembered my red speedboat and all the rest I had taken for granted. I thought of my parents—of my father who was by now certainly organizing a search party for me. And I remembered Gary's treachery; that was a score that needed settling.

It was different for Kelly and Sunyo. For them, going to a city meant a return to the island, to the stockade. My father might be able to do something for them, but it was not something which, in their shoes, one would like to bank on. The city a few hours' ride away was Southampton. Tomorrow afternoon I could be with the Sherrins.

I said, "I'd rather go back."

I did not glance at Kelly and Sunyo. Wild Jack looked at me, but his face was shadowed and I could not read his expression.

He said, "Your decision, lad. Free men can choose their futures." He put a hand on the shoulders of Kelly and Sunyo. "We've got two new men, anyway. And two are better than none!"

9

BY NOW I WAS ACCUSTOMED TO SLEEPING rough, and I was weary from all the activities of the day, but I did not sleep well that night. For a long time I lay awake and listened to the steady breathing of Kelly and Sunyo. In the morning I was tired and sluggish and morose.

For the last time I had breakfast with the outlaws. Tonight I would be eating city food, from Mrs. Sherrin's well-stocked freezer or maybe in a restaurant. I tried to think of what I might choose while I chewed on a hunk of gammon but could not summon up much interest in the prospect. So I imagined

Miranda sitting on the other side of the table from me and felt a little better.

Afterward we went along the forest trails southeast toward Southampton. I had the gray pony, Gibbon, on which I had learned to ride. He looked small and unimpressive beside Wild Jack's black gelding, Captain, but I had grown fond of him. He had tolerated my crude efforts very well. He was altogether amiable in temper and very sure-footed.

Wild Jack, Daniel, and Ben were in the party, together with Kelly and Sunyo and Joan. I had no idea why she had chosen to come, unless it was to be certain of getting rid of me. She had not said anything about my decision to go back to the city, but I had a fair notion of the thoughts that would be passing through her mind. I looked at her covertly as we rode over a patch of rough ground. She was not really bad looking, I supposed, unless you compared her with someone like Miranda.

We came at last to the edge of the forest and a sight of the highway. It looked strange and bleak after the green confusion of the trees. The empty road ran into the broad and equally empty circle which surrounded the town, and beyond that I saw the high gray wall of Southampton. Everything out there had a cold, smooth look.

I could still change my mind. Kelly and Sunyo would be pleased and so, I was fairly certain, would Wild Jack. With the parting so close I was beginning to realize how much I was going to miss the life I had recently been leading. Yet it would be stupid and silly to be influenced by thoughts like that. When you made a decision, you had to stick to it. An airship rose from behind the distant wall, and I thought of the other airship which would carry me back to London. I thought, too, with a quick and warming thrust of anger, of the surprise Gary would get when he saw me.

We all dismounted. I said good-bye to Kelly and Sunyo and wished them luck.

Kelly said, "Same to you, boss."

Sunyo's hand gripped mine. "We'll remember you."

I thanked the men in green for all their hospitality and help. Wild Jack said, "No need for thanks. All men are brothers in the Outlands." He smiled. "We wish you well in your city life."

I nodded, not wanting to talk. He took Gibbon's reins and said, "You could have kept him—we are well enough off for horses—but I doubt if it would be practicable in London. I doubt if he would enjoy the life either, being an Outlander born and bred. But there is something you can take to remember us by."

It was tied to his saddle, covered by a piece of cloth. He undid the cord and pulled the cloth away. He lifted up a small wicker cage holding a bird, a pigeon reddish-brown in plumage.

"Rusty!" I shook my head. "I can't take him. You said he was your favorite, your best bird."

"Birds don't last forever, any more than men. He's served his time and earned a soft retirement. You can build him a pretty cage, a golden one if you like, to end his days in. And think of your outlaw friends when you give him his seed." He shook hands. "Good-bye, lad."

Joan came from behind him. She said, "Good luck, Clive." That was the first time she had used my name—it had always been 'city boy.' "I shall miss you."

I was almost too surprised to do anything, but I put my hand out awkwardly. She ignored it; instead she reached forward quickly and kissed me.

"Good-bye."

• • •

I followed the highway toward Southampton's gate. No car passed me in either direction during the quarter of an hour it took me to reach it, but there was nothing unusual in that. Every year the roads were used less, and some people argued that they ought to be allowed to decay completely; airships provided adequate transport both for passengers and freight. For that matter, passenger traffic on the airships was declining, too. People were more and more inclined to remain in the city of their birth rather than go to the trouble of traveling to another which would be no better or, in fact, much different.

Cars were equipped with radio transmitters to beam a direct warning of their approach to the guard on duty, but there was also an auxiliary link with the gatehouse. I pressed the button and waited, knowing my image would be appearing on the screen inside, for examination by the guard. At last the gate slid open, and I walked inside.

The sergeant on duty looked at me closely and with suspicion. As he studied me, I became conscious of the figure I must cut. My clothes had been washed in the river and dried in the sun, with no mechanical press to provide them with city neatness. They were also badly torn in places.

He was a big man and fatter than he ought to be, heavily jowled, though he seemed to be only in his thirties. A few weeks in the Outlands, I thought, would melt away that surplus flesh. His manner showed the typical policeman's mistrust of the unusual. He snapped on his memocorder and said, "Right. Details. Name?" I told him. "Where do you come from?"

I was not going to tell the true story just yet; I needed to get in touch with my father first. I told him that I had gone out into the forest on a dare. That was something boys occasionally did, even though it was forbidden. Then I had got lost.

"Are you from this city?"

He probably knew most of the boys in the city. I shook my head.

"From London."

"You came seventy miles through the Outlands on your own?"

He was skeptical; it was not something which would have convinced me easily. I said, "I was given help."

"Help? *How?* Are you telling me you were helped by savages?"

Outlaws, I thought, not savages; but I had the sense not to say it. I nodded.

"They gave me food. And they were coming this way and let me travel with them."

"I should have thought they'd be more likely to cut your throat." He felt between his teeth with a fingernail. "It's a bit of a tall story. I suppose you don't know anyone in Southampton who would vouch for you?"

I was ready for that. "Mr. Sherrin. He's . . ."

"I know Mr. Sherrin." He looked less hostile, even impressed. Mr. Sherrin was obviously respected in police circles. He pointed to the visiphone.

"You can call him from here."

To my surprise and delight, Miranda came with her father to pick me up. I asked how she had managed to get away from school, and she told me it was a holiday, the anniversary of the birthday of the first president of the Southampton Council.

We traveled back in their car, a better one than I would have expected, scarcely inferior to my father's limousine. I was a bit surprised by their house, too, which was a mansion standing in impressive grounds. Mr. Sherrin did not say much in front of the chauffeur, and I did not volunteer anything except to ask about my parents: had they been very worried? He said they had and would be relieved to get news of me.

From time to time I glanced at Miranda, and she smiled back. Her hair was arranged in a new style, piled up in whorls over her head. It was pretty, but I wondered for the first time if the gold was real, then disliked myself for thinking it.

The Sherrins' butler was about Wild Jack's height and about his age; but there was nothing wild about him. He walked with a stoop, as though a small but heavy weight rested permanently on the back of his neck. Mr. Sherrin asked, when he opened the door for us, "Any messages, boy?"

Boy, I thought. The butler shook his head.

"No, master. No messages."

Mr. Sherrin said, "Come along into my study, Clive. We'd better have a talk. No, not you, Miranda. There'll be plenty of time for you and Clive to talk later."

She smiled and shrugged and went away. I followed Mr. Sherrin into his study, a large well-furnished room with a view across a wide lawn where a gardener was trundling a mower. There was a visiphone fitted on the desk and I said, "Could I call my father first? Since they've been worried."

"No point." He showed me a chair and sat down himself. "I called before we came to get you, but he wasn't available. I've left a message for him."

His face was gray, I thought, as well as his hair. His skin had a soft, tired look.

I said, "I could try my mother, then."

"I've done that, too. She's out. Don't worry. They'll call you here as soon as they can. Tell me what's been happening to you."

I told him, and he listened without interruption. He nodded in sympathy when I was indignant about the way I had been treated by the police and later on the island. It wasn't until I reached the part about our being found by the tribesmen and taken to Wild Jack that he started asking questions. He seemed quite interested in the outlaws.

I told him how well they had looked after us and how different the Outlands were from the stories about them. I explained that the savages were not really savage, while the outlaws, in their own way, were as civilized as we were.

Mr. Sherrin smiled. "You're very enthusiastic about them."

"There's no real reason, is there, why the world should be divided the way it is, with some people living in cities behind walls and others in the wilds? It doesn't really have to be like that?"

"It's a complicated question, but there's a lot in what you say." He pressed a button on his desk. "You look as though you could do with a bath and clean clothes. And something to eat."

I shook my head. "They fed us very well."

The butler came in. Mr. Sherrin said to him, "Show Master Clive to his room and see that he has everything he wants." He smiled. "When you've tidied up, you can have lunch with Miranda. I have to go out, but I'll see you later."

I was taken to a room on the first floor. The butler offered to carry Rusty's cage, but I refused. I put the cage down on a table near the window, from which there was a view across the city to the massed green of the Outlands beyond. The butler showed

me the bathroom and told me clothes would be sent up. He asked me if there was anything else I wanted.

"No, thank you, boy."

I spoke without thinking, falling back naturally into the use of the term. He showed no resentment, and, of course, there was no reason to think he felt any. There had always been masters and servants and always would be. It was part of the nature of things—no one's fault. All the same I was confused. I stared out the window toward the distant, different world I had just left.

But there was no point in brooding; the important thing was that I would soon be home. Something occurred to me. Mr. Sherrin had said both my parents were out when he called. There were several places my father might be, but if my mother were away from home at this time of day, she would almost certainly be at her ladies club at Blackfriars. I could visiphone her there.

I turned off the bath the butler had started running and headed downstairs. There was no one about. The door of Mr. Sherrin's study was open, and I heard voices inside. I was hesitating when I heard my name in a woman's voice—Mrs. Sherrin's.

"Even though he's not very bright," she said, "he's bound to start suspecting something soon. When he doesn't get a call from his parents, for instance."

Mr. Sherrin said, "We can stall him for an hour or two. I want Miranda to talk to him—that's why I hauled her out of school. It's this one who calls himself Wild Jack I'm interested in. I didn't want to ask him too many questions myself, but he'll talk to Miranda."

"That's not as important as the main issue," Mrs. Sherrin said. "Things are still tricky. Now that he's turned up like this . . ."

It was incredible at first, and then I thought it must be some kind of lunatic joke. But as they went on talking, it all fell into ugly but convincing shape, and I began to understand. Being picked up by the police and sent to the island had been no mistake. It had been done deliberately. And yet my part was only incidental; the real plot was directed against my father.

Plots and intrigues, I knew, were nothing unusual in city politics; it was one such that had resulted in Mr. Sherrin's banishment from London. In this case

the idea had been to involve me with a subversive group who were supposed to be agitating for improved conditions among the servants. Since I was his only son, this in itself would weaken my father's position, but there was also an ulterior motive. His impulsiveness was well known and would, it was hoped, provoke him to the kind of rash action which would enable his enemies to trip him up.

This was the explanation of my being denounced and taken to the island. I was to be kept there, well away from London, while a case was prepared against me. Then I would be put on trial, along with others. They were sure my father would take illegal action to free me, and when he did, they were ready to take counteraction to destroy him.

That was the word Mr. Sherrin used: "destroy." I had a feeling it was meant precisely. He was too big a man merely to be banished.

I tried to think clearly. I was supposed to be having a bath and changing. There was not much time before they would start looking for me, and I must not waste a second of it. If I could get as far as the wall. . . .

I turned to go, but realized as I did that someone

was coming through the hall toward me. It was Miranda. I saw the look in her face, uncertain and wary. The silly, irrelevant thought went through my head that I had been right about her hair—it was dyed, not natural.

And with that, I knew something else. I remembered the scene in the police building in London—that string of accusations from some informer who must have been present on the night of Brian's party. I had been sure it was Gary; now I was even more sure I had guessed wrong. Miranda had been there, too. It was Miranda who had told those lies.

Any lingering doubt I might have had went when she called out, "Father! Clive's out here. He's been listening at the door."

This time I was taken upstairs under the close escort of two servants, and the door of the room was locked after me. I went to the window and looked out. The ground was more than twenty feet below, and the garden was full of servants working. There was no chance of escape.

I stared over the city at the Outlands and thought of Kelly and Sunyo and what a fool I'd been. They

were free, with Wild Jack, while I had come back to treachery and the prospect of imprisonment—the prospect also of being the means by which my father's enemies would bring him down.

I felt afraid and sick and angry. I was angry with the Sherrins but even more with my own stupidity. Having been lucky enough once to get out of a trap, I had walked right back into it. I knew what would happen. I would be taken back to the island, and they would make quite sure I had no opportunity of escaping again. They would keep me there until they were ready to put me on show in London.

A car drove through the grounds and stopped by the front door. Two policemen got out. Mr. Sherrin must have called them in, anxious to get me off his hands and in proper custody now that I knew the truth of the situation. He didn't want the risk of keeping me in his house.

I turned and saw the cage on the table. They would never let me take Rusty to the island. What do you do with an unwanted pigeon—wring its neck?

Even if I had thrown away my own freedom, I could give Rusty his. I took the cage over to the window and opened the little door in the side.

Rusty did not want to come out at first. I put my fingers inside, and he pecked them. So I lifted him out and he sat undisturbed on my hand.

"Off you go," I said. "Back to your forest."

With a flick of my wrist I threw him forward, and he dipped and then flew up into the sky. I saw him circle once and afterward fly in a straight line across the town and out over the wall. I watched until he was out of sight.

10

THE POLICE BUILDING IN SOUTHAMPTON WAS
smaller than the one in London but very similar
in other respects. The room to which I was
taken was almost identical with that in which I had
been quizzed about the party. There were two
policemen again, and again one did the talking while
the other listened.

The questions were all about Wild Jack and the
outlaws. This confirmed what I had guessed from
the conversation between the Sherrins—that the
men in green were taken a good deal more seriously
than contemptuous remarks about savages might

indicate. It only reinforced the intention I had already formed not to tell them anything which could possibly be of value.

The interrogation was amiable to begin with but became distinctly less friendly when my answers proved unsatisfactory. No, I had no idea of the direction we had come in getting to Southampton. And no, I had no idea how many men were in Wild Jack's band. More than twenty? More than fifty? A hundred? I shrugged helplessly.

The policeman doing the talking—like the one in the gatehouse, a bit flabby, I thought—advised me to be more cooperative. In the morning I would be taken back to the island. That was no concern of theirs—it was his turn to shrug—but they were in a position where they could help me. I was due for severe punishment—the stockade for a certainty— because of the escape. It might make a considerable difference in the way I was treated if I went back with a commendation from them for doing my civic duty while in custody. An adverse report, on the other hand, was likely to make a bad situation worse.

I just went on acting dumb, and in the end they got tired. The talking policeman remarked that I

might be more sensible after a night in a cell; I would be interrogated again before being taken to the airship.

The cell was on the second floor—a small gray cube of a room with an iron bed fixed to the wall and a sanitary unit at one end. Apart from that, nothing. I sat wretchedly on the bed while the afternoon light darkened into dusk. The single window of the cell did not open and was at least thirty feet above the concrete pavement. Even if I smashed the glass and got out, I would break a leg in jumping or more probably kill myself.

From this small window, too, I could see the forest beyond the city's wall. It was gray in the evening light—gray like the walls of the cell. But the morning light would turn it green again; Kelly and Sunyo would wake up to sunlight bursting through a screen of leaves. I wondered what they would be doing tomorrow: fishing, perhaps, or riding. There was a chance, Wild Jack had said, that they might be able to go with the men on the next deer hunt.

I thought of Joan, too, and then of Miranda. Acting dumb to the policemen was really only appropriate. It was stupidity which had put me here.

Supper was brought on a tray: some kind of concentrate with a slice of tasteless bread and a synthetic drink to wash it down. I would rather have had Wild Jack's bread and water. I ate and drank, to pass the time as much as anything, and afterward lay on the bed.

Unhappy and unhopeful thoughts chased each other's tails in continual miserable chase through my mind. The cell was lit by a single light in the center of the ceiling, irritating both by its dimness and the fact that it could not be turned off. I stared at it, or at the darkening square of the window, and tried to go to sleep, but eventually I abandoned hope of that, too.

In the end, though, tiredness overcame me.

My sleep was disturbed by dreams, of which I remembered nothing except that they were the sort you would not choose to remember. I woke out of one particularly unpleasant one, hearing my name called. It must have been part of the dream, I decided, feeling sweat cold on my body. Then, properly awake, I heard it again.

The light still burned in the ceiling, but beyond the window there was moonlight. The call had come from there. It came again: "Clive. . . ."

The voice was Wild Jack's. But that was impossible. I jumped off the bed and ran across to look out.

Horsemen, half a dozen or more, were milling about in the street. I broke the window with my elbow and heard glass tinkle down the wall. Shoving my head through the jagged hole, I called back, "It's me, Jack! I'm here."

Faces stared up in the moonlight, and I saw a familiar black beard. Wild Jack shouted, "Are you happy there, lad, or would you rather come with us?"

His teeth gleamed as he laughed. I felt exhilarated, but it was a long way down to the ground. I cried, "I'm locked in."

Instead of replying, Wild Jack took a coil of rope from his saddle and tossed the free end up toward me. His throw was accurate enough, but I missed it the first time. He sent it snaking up the wall again, and I caught it.

"Make it fast," he said.

The bed was the only piece of furniture, but at least it was fixed to the wall. I tied the end of the rope around a leg of the bed in a double clove hitch, one of the things I had learned among the outlaws. I went back to the window.

"I'm ready."

"Down you come, then."

I knocked the rest of the glass out of the frame and eased myself through, holding onto the rope. I slid down, burning my hands a bit by going too fast. Wild Jack hauled me onto the horse's back behind him, with one hand.

To his men he said, "Right! Back to the gate."

The sound of hooves echoed loud in the streets. I saw a few heads looking from behind windows, but no one came out, I wondered why the police on duty at the police building had not done something. How had Wild Jack got into the town, for that matter, and how did he propose to get out?

As we got near the gate, I suddenly saw figures of uniformed men in the streets ahead of us and a moment later heard the sharp crack of guns. In reply there were other sounds: a soft swish of arrows through the air. I saw one policeman drop, collapsing onto the shaft of the arrow which went through his chest, and others scurry back into the shadows. Someone else fired from the open door of the gatehouse. Wild Jack's arrow took him, and he did not fire again. Seeing him fall, I had a good idea what had happened to the men from the police building.

Jack rode his horse up to the open door of the gatehouse. He said to the guard at the control panel, "Open up."

There was another arrow in his bow. The guard did not argue but pressed a button, and there was the hum of the gates sliding apart.

Jack gestured to the guard. "Now, out."

We rode away from the city, a few futile shots fired in our rear. As we crossed the empty land outside the wall, I looked back and saw it, high and gleaming in the moonlight. It did not seem possible that the outlaws could have ridden in there and brought me out. And yet it had happened. This was not dream but reality. I heard the thud of hooves, felt the ripple of the horse's stride beneath me.

We were already close by the forest, following the line of the highway to the west. I asked Wild Jack, "What made you come for me?"

"We had a messenger."

I was confused. "A messenger?"

"Rusty returned to his box."

"He carried no message."

"We believed he did. You might have let him go

because you thought him too much trouble to keep. It seemed more likely that you were the one in trouble."

"And just because of that you rode into the city?"

Wild Jack laughed. "For that and our amusement! Life has been quiet lately."

I still could not grasp it. "But they must have opened the gate for you."

"We know more about their ways than they imagine. A police car drives in every night from the west at the same time. We rode up close to the wall beforehand. They did not see us, partly because of the dark and partly because they keep a poor watch."

That was true. I had not been seen approaching either, and that had been in daylight.

Wild Jack went on. "When they opened up for the car, they opened up for us. We only had to follow it in."

That covered one out of a heap of improbabilities. I said, "How did you know where to find me?"

"We didn't know which cell—that was why we had to shout for you. But the police building was the obvious place to look if you were in trouble."

"How did you know which was the police building?"

"I've told you—we know more about the cities than you think."

"You were talking about watching from the outside—cars coming in and so on. It's not the same."

"Maybe we have friends inside the walls."

"Friends?" Despite all that had happened, that shocked me a bit. "You mean, traitors to the cities?"

"Can a slave be a traitor?"

"The servants?" Even that was a staggerer. "They send out information to you?"

He laughed again. "You are still a bit new to be told all our secrets! Perhaps you can see now why we put recruits to the test."

We rode for a time in silence. I said at last, "I still don't see how you dared do it—with bows and arrows against guns."

"We had surprise on our side. And they are city men." He spoke with contempt. "They keep a poor watch, and they are not accustomed to shocks. It was night and they were asleep or half asleep, frightened by their own shadows. Yes, they have guns, but we can shoot our arrows straighter. And at close quarters a bow is a match for any gun."

He turned Captain in toward the forest, the rest of the troop following. He said: "They're soft. They've held power for a long time—power from their machines and power over their servants. Their lives are easy and untroubled. They know about the savages, of course, but the savages live on the other side of the wall, in the Outlands. They have no reason to be afraid of them.

"Then suddenly there is a real enemy, inside their city at night. They are surprised first, then dismayed, soon scared witless. And fearful men have lost the fight before they begin it."

I could see it might be true: the converse, also. A brave man has half won his fight before he starts, even against heavy odds. But the heavier the odds, the braver he has got to be.

I thought of my parents as we rode through the forest trails. As the excitement of the rescue faded, I realized sharply that I was not going to see them for a very long time—perhaps not ever again. It was a miserable thought, but at least carried one consolation: I could not now be used as a weapon against my father. His enemies would probably still try to pull him down, but they would not find it easy. I remembered the set of his jaw, his exuberant laugh. No, not at all easy.

We reached the camp as moonlight was giving way to the light of dawn. People came out of the huts at the sound of our arrival. I saw Kelly and Sunyo, grinning in welcome, and slid down from my seat behind Wild Jack.

Joan was there, too. Wild Jack called down to her, "Here he is, daughter! I've brought him back, as I promised. With luck we'll make an outlaw of him."

Read on for a peek at another adventure
from John Christopher!

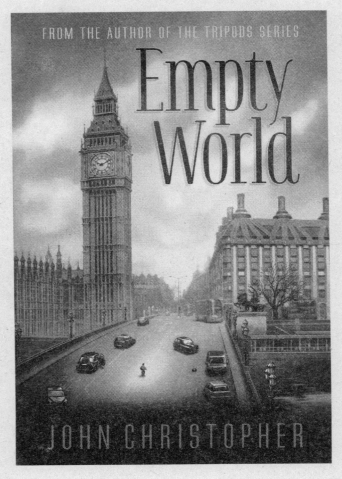

FROM THE AUTHOR OF THE TRIPODS SERIES

Empty
World

JOHN CHRISTOPHER

T HEY WERE DRIVING ALONG THE MOTORWAY on a bright sunny morning, everyone happy. While Neil's father drove, his mother was telling him something about a dance at the golf club. Amanda and Andy were arguing, but amiably, about a pop programme they had watched on TV. Grandpa and Grandma were admiring the countryside, he pointing out a view that attracted him and she agreeing. Neil himself was silent, engrossed in a strange but satisfying feeling of well-being. He tried to work out what had given rise to it, but could not. It being end of term, the try he had scored in the junior House final, the prospect of summer and the cricket season ahead? Or perhaps just this journey.

He could not decide, but it did not matter. He was relaxing in the enjoyment of that, too—it not mattering—when he heard his mother's small gasping cry and looked up to see it: the monstrous hulk of the heavy lorry and trailer jack-knifing across the road in front of them, looming up and up. . . . Then screams, and blackness, and he woke up sweating, his fingers digging into the bed clothes that were wrapped tightly round him.

Neil thought about the dream later that day, as he walked across the churchyard on his way to catch the bus to school. It had been full of inaccuracies and impossibilities, the way dreams were. Not a sunny morning, but a dull rain-bleared afternoon. Not a motorway, but the A21, a few miles south of the Tonbridge bypass. And, of course, Grandpa and Grandma had not been there. The Rover was a roomy car, but not that roomy; and besides, the object of the journey had been to spend the weekend with them at Winchelsea.

But the rest—his mother's soft cry, the sight of the monster twisting incredibly across their path . . . was that the way it had been? He had no way of knowing, no recollection of the time between setting out from the house in Dulwich and waking in a hospital bed with a nurse, young, dark and pretty, bending over and smiling and telling him he was all right, and not to worry. He had wondered what she was talking about, and asked what he was doing there; and she had told him again not to worry about anything but to lie back and rest, and he would have visitors very soon.

Neil walked through the crumbling stone archway into the empty shell of what had been the nave of the church before it was destroyed in the French wars. That was nearly seven hundred years ago. Winchelsea then had been a thriving town, recently rebuilt here on its hill after the sea swallowed up old Winchelsea— like its sister-town, Rye, a brash newcomer to the company of the Cinque Ports and hopeful of out-stripping its seniors in trade and prosperity. But the sea which destroyed the first port had capriciously moved away from the second, remaining as no more than a mocking gleam on the horizon.

So the hopes had come to nothing, and the traders had gone with the sea. Only a few squares were left of the grid pattern which had made the town a contem-porary showplace of planning; and those were occu-pied by sleepy houses, fronted by lawns and flowers, three or four small shops, a couple of pubs. There had been no point in rebuilding the nave of the church, and the New Gate, which had marked the southern limits of Winchelsea, and through which one summer morning late in the thirteenth century the French had been treacherously admitted, stood now over a muddy lane, nearly a mile out in the country, surrounded by grazing sheep.

There were not many young people in Winchelsea. It was a place for retirement—that was why his grandparents had come to live in it. And in the past, although he had liked visiting them, Neil had felt a kind of impatience. Nothing happened here or was likely to happen, beyond the slow change of the seasons. He looked at the white facades of the houses making up the sides of the great square of the churchyard. Even the post-war ones had an appearance of having been there forever.

He thought of the dream, and then of Grandpa coming to his bedside in the hospital. He had asked Neil how he was, and nodded when he said he had a headache.

"A touch of concussion, but they tell me you're sound in wind and limb."

His grandfather, a Civil Servant until his retirement, was a tall thin man, with a long face lengthened further by a white pointed beard. Although he liked them both, Neil preferred him to his grandmother because he never fussed and talked directly, paying little regard to differences in age. His manner had always been calm and easy. He was trying to look calm and easy now, but not managing. Neil asked him:

"What happened?"

"What have they told you?"

"Nothing. I've not been awake long."

"There was a smash. You don't remember it?"

His tone was even but Neil was conscious of the strain behind it. He thought of them all setting out together after lunch—Amanda insisting on going back to say another goodbye to Prinny, the cat, and worrying in case Mrs. Redmayne might not remember to come in and feed him. . . . He said sharply:

"Where's Mummy? Is she in hospital, too?" He realized, for the first time properly, that the other beds in the ward were occupied by strangers. "And Amanda, and Andy?"

"They're all right. Don't worry, Neil."

There had been a hesitation, though; very slight,

but enough to make the reassurance meaningless. And what he said was meaningless, anyway; because if they had been all right his mother would have been here, beside his bed. He said, hearing his voice echo as though far off:

"All of them?" He stared up at his grandfather. "Dad, as well?"

"They're all right," his grandfather repeated.

He did not need the sight of the tear rolling down the wrinkled cheek to give the lie. Nor did he resent it, knowing the lie was meant to help him, to ease him back into a world that had shattered and changed. But he could not go on looking at another human being. He turned and buried his head in the pillow, immobile, believing and not believing, while his grandfather's voice went on and on and he heard it without listening, an empty noise.

There were others from the Comprehensive waiting at the bus stop. He knew them slightly, and nodded to one or two, but did not engage in conversation. There had been the curiosity one could expect over a newcomer but he had done little to satisfy it; and when the suspicion which was also inevitable had hardened into something more like hostility, he had not minded.

It was a big change from London, and Dulwich College. There had been a talk with his grandfather about that. It seemed the Head had offered to find him one of the few boarding places, and his grandfather had put the proposition to him: he could choose between taking it, and keeping a continuity in school at least, or going as a day boy to the Comprehensive School in Rye.

"Your home's with us now, Neil," Grandpa had said, "and we're very glad to have you—glad for our own sakes. But we're old, and a bit dull, and so is Winchelsea. You might find it better to carry on at Dulwich where there are people you know—chaps your own age."

"No, I'll stay here."

"If you're thinking of the fees, that's not important. You know. . . ."

"No."

He said it brusquely. He had heard his grandparents talking one evening, quietly when they thought he was asleep. There would be a lot of money coming his way. His father, an insurance executive, had himself been more than amply insured. The sole survivor of the family was going to be rich.

The new school was very different from the old, but a large part of the difference, he realized, lay in himself. At Dulwich he had made plenty of friends— more than Andy who, though a year older, was more reserved. And Andy had not been much interested in sports, while he played most games reasonably well.

He had taken part in a couple of cricket games at Rye, and not done badly. But he had kept to himself and the other players, after one or two small overtures, had let him get on with it. It had been the same in school generally. Although it was never mentioned, he guessed the story of what had happened, the reason for his coming here, had got around. He had had one or two pitying glances from girls, and once found a conversation abruptly switched off as he entered a class-room. But no questions were asked, and he volunteered no information.

So he had made no friends, but did not mind it; nor did he miss the ones he had left behind. It was not that he brooded over the disaster. It surprised him to what extent he was able to put it out of his mind; and in spite of occasional lurching moments of fear and sickness, he did not feel particularly unhappy.

He had an idea it would not have been so easy in London. The impatience he had once felt for the slowness and dullness of the little town had been replaced by a kind of contentment. It was good that nothing happened, and that the most usual sight was of an old man or woman creeping along on some unhurried errand. He liked the quiet empty evenings, with the darkness lit only by chinks of light from cosy sitting rooms, and the single street lamp on the corner.

The others who were at the bus stop had collected into a group and were talking and laughing. He did not know what the subject of conversation was, and did not care. He thought of his dream again, and felt sweat cold down his back, but both dream and reality seemed far away. As the bus came growling down the road from Hastings, through an avenue of leafy green, he found himself whistling. He realized it was the tune Amanda had been so crazy about the last few weeks, but went on.

. . .

In general the work seemed easier in Neil's new school, but perhaps because of that less interesting. An exception was Biology, taught by a small stocky man with a Scottish accent and a tendency to range widely round his subject. Today they were dealing with cell structures, and Mr Dunhill moved on to a discussion of the ageing process. There was some evidence, he pointed out, for believing that ageing was caused by the increasing inability of cells to remember the functions laid down for them in the genetic blueprint, a sort of cellular amnesia.

Someone asked if that meant that if something could be done to improve the memory of cells the ageing process could be halted—even reversed? Did it mean people might be able to live forever, barring accidents?

"Well, no, I wouldn't hazard that."

Mr Dunhill rubbed his palms together in front of his chest, a characteristic gesture. He went on:

"But there's an interesting example in the opposite direction, in that epidemic they had in India, a few months back."

The Calcutta Plague, it had been called, because

that was where the first cases had occurred. It had swept through northern India, killing hundreds of thousands, and then died out. Neil remembered his father and mother discussing it one evening when he came downstairs after finishing his prep. Their preoccupation, he recalled, had given him the chance of slipping out to a friend's house, without their realizing how late it was.

"You'll remember there were two phases of the disease," Mr Dunhill said. "Initially there was a fever, followed by recovery and a symptomless period varying between ten days and three weeks. That was followed by a general deterioration of bodily functions, leading to collapse and death.

"The striking thing was that the second phase strongly resembled an accelerated ageing process. It mimicked a rare disorder called progeria, specifically the Hutchinson-Gilford syndrome, in which children grow old before they grow up. There was a well-known case of a child in Brazil, who at six months had adult teeth already yellowing, at two years white hair, thinning on top, and who died at ten of hardening of the arteries.

"Fortunately in this case it was not the young

who were affected but the old, chiefly the very old. Mostly the victims were over sixty. There were one or two cases as young as the middle forties, and the results there were much more striking: wrinkling of skin, whitening of hair roots, calcium loss, athero-sclerosis. It was as though they were racing towards the grave, instead of indulging in that slow crawl which satisfies us normal geriatrics."

Mr Dunhill was in his fifties. It was probably as much as forty years since he had sat in a class-room, listening to someone as old as he was now. Was the joke about being a geriatric as light-hearted, Neil wondered, as it seemed? People died: he had come to know that in the last few weeks in a way he had never known before. And they must fear it, he supposed, more and more as the inevitability drew closer.

"It's a tenable explanation," Mr Dunhill went on, "that the Calcutta virus attacked the individual cells in such a way as to inhibit or destroy that memory function we have been talking about. The victims quite literally died of nothing except old age."

"They were old already, though."

That was someone called Barker, a gangling boy

with an almost perpetual silly grin. Mr Dunhill looked at him with distaste.

"Yes, they were, weren't they? And they were only Indians, after all. Nothing to cause us concern. Now let's get back to the mechanism of mitosis."

There was a girl in the class called Ellen, pretty in a fair, frail way. Neil had noticed her chiefly in the company of Bob Hendrix, who was more conspicuous. He was heavily built and had a loud aggressive voice. His hair was bright red, and he usually wore a canary-yellow waistcoat. His father was a prominent Rye tradesman, and he clearly thought deference was due to him on that account.

Hendrix went home for lunch but Ellen, like Neil, stayed at school. On this day she sat near him, and made what appeared to be friendly if timid overtures. He answered her civilly, but without enthusiasm. She persisted, though, and afterwards found him and spoke to him more directly.

"Is it true?" He looked at her. "About your family all being killed?"

It was something he had reckoned on happening

but had hoped, with the lapse of time, might not. It was not that he dreaded the reference—more a feeling of embarrassment in advance. Now it had happened, though, he found it did not bother him. She seemed sympathetic rather than curious—a nice girl, probably.

At any rate, although he did not volunteer much information, he did not snub her. She went on, in a small soft voice, saying what a terrible thing it was, and he found he did not mind that, either.

It was something, she said, which had always been a nightmare with her. She had imagined it hundreds of times, and it had pursued her in dreams. She mostly thought of it as happening at school—of someone coming in to the class and telling her to report to the Headmaster, of going into his study and seeing his face, much graver than usual. And then being told—it was always both of them killed together, usually in a car smash.

Once launched she needed no encouragement to go on. She told him about her life at home, and he was a little surprised. She was an only child. Her father, a plasterer, was very strict—he did not allow her out later than ten in the evening, half past nine in winter. Her mother, it seemed, was ill a great deal. She had to get her own breakfast in the morning, and do housework before she came to school.

It did not strike Neil as the sort of home life one would be particularly terrified to lose; nor her parents as justifying such anxious devotion. Her life in fact seemed fairly wretched compared with the one he had known in Dulwich. Yet he had never had the sort of fears she described. Did that mean he had failed to appreciate what he'd got? He felt a vague guilt, and had a panicky moment of wondering if that was why it had happened—if the God in whom he mostly didn't believe had read his ungrateful mind, and casually sent down destruction.

But he had no time to brood on it because at that point Hendrix joined them. He ignored Neil, and said to Ellen:

"I thought I told you I'd see you outside the library at half past?"

His tone was truculent. Ellen did not reply, but looked at Neil. He had an impulse to tell Hendrix to push off, but it was easily controlled.

Hendrix said: "And haven't I told you about hanging about with other fellers?"

He was not just truculent, but bullying and contemptuous. Ellen looked at Neil again, in direct appeal this time.

Neil had no fear of the other. He was bigger, possibly stronger, but Neil was fairly sure he was no boxer while he had done quite a bit. If this had happened a couple of months ago he knew what he would have done—told Hendrix to shut up, or he'd sort him out.

He supposed really that was what he ought to do now, but he could not be bothered. Neither the girl nor Hendrix meant enough to be worth his getting involved. The girl, after all, had chosen Hendrix in the past, or let herself be chosen by him. It was not his concern, but if he fought Hendrix and beat him it might become so. Her eyes stayed on his face, but he said nothing.

Hendrix said, openly contemptuous of Neil as well: "Come on. Leave this London wet. It's Geography first and I didn't have time to do any prep last night. We'll go and get yours."

Neil watched them go off together. He was a bit surprised he could feel so detached about it.

• • •

He walked back through the churchyard in the late afternoon. The air was windless, warm for early summer, and the crab apple trees were loaded with blossom. Although many of the graves were old, the inscriptions on the stones rendered illegible by time and weather, some were new, and he passed two graves freshly mounded with flowers. The churchyard represented one of the few ongoing enterprises the town still possessed, the only one really.

Neil thought of Ellen and her nightmares, and wondered about them. Perhaps they did not stem, as he had assumed, from love of her parents, but the reverse. Perhaps that was why the daydream was so persistent.

He wondered too what the future would bring, for her and Hendrix. Most likely nothing: they were very young and there was no reason to suppose anything permanent, like marriage, would come of it. Though it might, of course. Hendrix enjoyed bullying, and Neil had an idea that a part of Ellen, at least, liked being bullied. Maybe they *would* marry, and she could change her nightmares to imagining her husband being killed.

Again his thoughts surprised him. He looked up

at the sky, nearly cloudless, where—he was fairly sure again—no invisible vindictive God lurked, reading minds and fashioning thunderbolts to toss down. The church was grey and squat, brooding over its generations of worshippers. All around were the quiet houses with, at this moment, not a person in sight. A car revved up the High Street and roared on towards Hastings, leaving velvety silence behind.

Rye was a quiet town after London, but a Babylon compared with Winchelsea. He thought again how glad he was to be here, but thought that even here there were too many people. It would be nice to live on a desert island, with only a parrot for company. Though the parrot wasn't really necessary, either: the sound of the surf or the wind in the palms would be company enough.

His grandmother came out of the kitchen as he let himself in at the front door. She fussed him as usual, and he accepted it as usual, but refused her offer to make him a snack. She was a great believer in nourishment, and seemed to regard the day in school at Rye as roughly equivalent to an ascent of Everest. In the end he escaped on the double plea of not being hungry and having heavy Physics prep to do. She believed in prep as well, though she thought he worked too hard.

That wasn't true, in fact; he was still coasting for the most part, after Dulwich. He worked away steadily, though, glad to have something to occupy his mind so completely but undemandingly. Apart from Physics, there was English and History . . . witches putting the frighteners on Macbeth, Judge Jeffreys decorating the west country with gibbeted rebels. Violent death was something you might as well get used to; it had been around a long time. And only a fool looked for explanations of justifications.

When he had finished he sat for a time, looking out. His room was at the top of the house and quite big. It ran from the front of the house to the back; his bed was under one window, and the desk at which he sat under the opposite one. This looked over the street, if anything so green and flowery could be called a street. Someone drove a car up, and parked it. Mrs Mellor from over the road passed slowly along his field of vision, and disappeared. A tabby cat succeeded her, and all was quiescence again.

Below and faintly he heard the theme music of BBC television news. He might as well go down and watch as not.

In the sitting room his grandfather and grand-mother were in their accustomed armchairs, with the third between them left empty for him. Neil stopped in the doorway, to see if there was anything interesting on. It was only something about the Calcutta Plague starting up again, this time in Karachi.